Esther's Inheritance

Sándor Márai was born in Kassa, in the Austro-Hungarian Empire, in 1900, and died in San Diego, California, in 1989. He rose to fame as one of the leading literary novelists in Hungary in the 1930s. Profoundly anti-fascist, he survived World War II, but persecution by the Communists drove him from the country in 1948. He went into exile, first in Italy, then in the United States.

Esther's Inheritance

SÁNDOR MÁRAI

*Translated from the Hungarian
by George Szirtes*

PICADOR

First published 2008 by Alfred A. Knopf,
a division of Random House, Inc., New York

First published in Great Britain 2009 by Picador

First published in paperback 2009 by Picador
an imprint of Pan Macmillan Ltd
Pan Macmillan, 20 New Wharf Road, London N1 9RR
Basingstoke and Oxford
Associated companies throughout the world
www.panmacmillan.com

Originally published in 1939 in Budapest, Hungary as
Eszter hagyatéka by Révai

ISBN 978-0-330-50407-2

1 3 5 7 9 8 6 4 2

A CIP catalogue record for this book is available
from the British Library.

Printed and bound in the UK by
CPI Mackays, Chatham ME5 8TD

Visit **www.picador.com** to read more about all our books
and to buy them. You will also find features, author interviews and
news of any author events, and you can sign up for e-newsletters
so that you're always first to hear about our new releases.

Esther's Inheritance

I

I don't know what else God has in store for me. But before I die I want to write down what happened the day Lajos visited me for the last time and robbed me. I have been waiting three years to set this down. Now I feel an irresistible voice urging me on, insisting I should record the events of that day—and everything I know about Lajos—because it is my duty to do so and because I don't have much time. There's no mistaking such a voice. That is why I obey it, in God's name.

I am no longer young nor healthy and soon I must die. Am I still afraid of dying? . . . That Sunday when Lajos visited us for the last time, I was, among other things, cured of my fear of death. Maybe time, which has not spared me, maybe memory, which is almost as ruthless as time, maybe some peculiar grace that, as my faith teaches, is sometimes granted the undeserving and the willful, maybe simply experience and old age enable me now to gaze on death with equanimity. Life has been extraordinarily kind to me, and, just as extraordinarily, it has robbed me of everything . . . what else can happen? Die I must, because that's how things are, and because I have fulfilled my duties.

I realize that's a big word to use, and now that I see it written down I feel a little scared. It's a haughty word that I shall have to answer for sometime in front of someone. How long was it before I recognized my duty and how I resisted it, screaming and protesting most desperately, before I gave in. The first time I felt death might be salvation was when I knew that death was resolution and peace. Life alone is struggle and humiliation. And what a struggle it was! Who ordered it, and why was it impossible to avoid? I did all I could to escape it. But my foe pursued me. Now I know he could do nothing about it: we are bound to our enemies, nor can they escape us.

2

*I*f I want to be honest—and what point in writing this if I am not?—I must confess that nowhere in my life and actions can I find the least trace of that biblical fury or passion, not even of the hardness and decisiveness, that seemed to strike strangers when it came to my views about Lajos or my personal fate. "I must do my duty!"—what a firm, declamatory expression. We live . . . then one day we notice that we have "done" or "not done" our duty. I have started to think that the great, decisive moments that broadly govern our lives are far less conscious at the time than they seem later when we are reminiscing and taking stock. By that time I had not seen Lajos for twenty years, and I thought myself inured against my memories. Then one day I received his telegram, which was like an opera libretto, just as theatrical, as dangerously childish and false, as everything he had said and written to others twenty years before . . . It was so much like a declaration, so full of promises, so clearly and transparently false, false! I went out to Nunu in the garden, the telegram in my hand, stood on the veranda, and loudly announced the news.

"Lajos is coming back!"

What would my voice have sounded like? It is unlikely that I was screaming with joy. I must have spoken like a sleepwalker suddenly woken out of her sleep. I had been sleepwalking for twenty years. For twenty years I had been walking at the edge of a precipice, neatly balanced, calm and smiling. Now I had been awoken and knew the truth. But I no longer felt dizziness. There is something calming about the sense of reality, whether of life or death. Nunu was binding the roses. She looked up at me from below, from a depth, under the deep roses, blinking in the sunlight, aged and calm.

"Well, of course," she said.

She carried on binding.

"When?" she asked.

"Tomorrow," I answered.

"Good," she said. "I will lock away the silver."

I started to laugh. But Nunu remained serious. Later

she sat down next to me on the concrete bench and read the telegram. "We will arrive in a car," wrote Lajos. From the rest we concluded he was bringing his children. "There will be five of us," the telegram continued. Chicken, milk, cream, thought Nunu. Who were the other two? we wondered. "We'll stay till the evening," the telegram went on to announce, followed by the kind of awful fancy talk Lajos could never resist, not even in a telegram. "Five people," said Nunu, "arriving in the morning to leave in the evening." Her pale old lips moved soundlessly as she counted and calculated. She was working out the cost of dinner and supper. Having done so, she said:

"I knew he'd come back sometime. But he dare not come alone now! He's bringing support, children and strangers. But there's nothing here anymore."

We sat in the garden and looked at each other. Nunu thinks she knows everything about me. And maybe she does know the truth, that simple ultimate truth we dress up in so many rags all our lives. I have always found Nunu's "omniscience" a little insulting. But she had been so good to me, and her goodness was so wise, so dry and uncomplicated. Eventually I always gave in to her. In those last years, when my life seemed to have been shrouded in an invisible damp mist, she was the torch by whose weak and gentle light I could guide my

steps. I knew the visit was unlikely to have truly dangerous, terrifying consequences, just as I knew that her
suggestion, on reading the first few words of the
telegram, that the silver be locked away was a joke.
That's an exaggeration, I thought. Nunu is teasing me.
And I knew at the same time that in the end, at the last
minute, Nunu would in fact lock away the silver, and
that later still, once the silver was forgotten, when we
discussed the whole thing, the thing that could not be
hidden, Nunu would be somewhere nearby with her
keys, in her best black dress, with her wrinkles, with her
silent, observant caution. But I also knew that when
that moment came I would be beyond all mortal help,
even Nunu's.

But it was pointless "knowing" all this; so all of a
sudden my mood lifted as if nothing threatened me. I
remember, I was joking with Nunu. We were sitting in
the garden listening to the intoxicated hum of late-
autumnal wasps, talking quietly and for a long time
of Lajos and the children, as well as of Vilma, my dead
sister. Our seat was in front of the house, under the window behind whose shutters Mother had died twenty-
five years before. In front of us were the lime trees and
Father's apiary, but it was all empty now. Nunu didn't
like messing about with the hives, and one day we sold
all eighteen colonies. It was September, gentle, mild

days. We sat there with that familiar sense of security that smacks partly of shipwreck and partly of happiness without desire. Come on now, I thought, what is there left for Lajos to take away? . . . The silver? Ridiculous idea: what were a few bent silver spoons worth? I calculated that Lajos would have passed fifty now, in fact he would have been fifty-three in the summer. It was unlikely that one could help him with silver spoons. If this kind of thing did help, let him take them. Nunu must have been thinking something similar. Then she gave a sigh and went into the house, only turning round on the veranda.

"Be careful not to spend too much time alone with him. Invite Laci, Tibor, and Uncle Endre to lunch too, just as you do every other Sunday when you come together to fool about with spirits. Lajos has always been frightened of Endre, I do believe he owes him something. Remember, is there anyone to whom he does not owe anything?" she asked, and started laughing.

"They have all forgotten," I said, and began to laugh myself.

I was already defending him. What could I do? He was the only man I ever loved.

3

*T*he telegram that brought news of disaster and delight had arrived on Saturday about noon. I can only faintly remember the afternoon and evening before Lajos's arrival. No. Nunu was right: I was no longer frightened of Lajos. We can be frightened by those we love or hate, by someone who is very good or quite ruthless or had quite deliberately betrayed us. But Lajos had never been awful to me: true, he wasn't good, either, in the sense school textbooks describe goodness. Did he betray me? No, I never felt betrayed by him. Certainly, he lied: he lied the way the wind howls, with a certain natural energy, in high spirits. He could tell the most wonderful lies. For example, he lied that he loved me, only me. Then he married my little sister, Vilma. Though later I became convinced that he hadn't planned all this, it wasn't a plot or a conspiracy, there was nothing intentional about it: Lajos never did anything deliberately wicked. He told me he loved me—and I don't doubt he meant it, even now—but he happened to marry Vilma, maybe because she was prettier, maybe because that day the wind happened to be blowing from the east, or maybe because that was what Vilma wanted. He never said why.

That night before the expected arrival of Lajos—it would be the last time in this life, as I well knew—I stayed up a long time arranging various mementos, preparing for his visit, and reading his old letters before falling asleep. Even today I believe, it is a superstition of mine—and reading his old letters I felt this once again with particular certainty and force—that Lajos had some hidden source of power, that he was like those little streams you find on high mountains that wind aimlessly down the slopes and disappear without a trace in the depths of a cave. No one used or directed that power. Now, reading over his letters the night before he came back to haunt me, I marveled at the fierce workings of this aimless energy. In each of his letters he addressed me with power enough to move anyone—especially a highly sensitive woman—indeed, whole crowds, even masses. It wasn't that he had anything particularly "significant" to say, nor did I detect any particular literary talent in his ideas: his epithets were scrappy, his style undisciplined—but his manner, the voice audible in every line of his writing, was unmistakably his and his alone! He was always writing about the truth, about some imagined truth that he had just realized and urgently wanted me to know.

He never wrote about his feelings, not even his plans, instead he described the town where he happened to be staying so vividly the reader could immediately see the streets and the room where Lajos was writing the letter, could hear the voices of people who had said something clever or amusing the day before. On top of this he would lay out the great idea that was currently demanding his attention, and all in such miraculously authentic terms that everything seemed larger than life. It was just that—and even this tin-eared reader could sense it—none of it was true, or rather it was all true but not as Lajos wrote it. His description of the town was as scrupulously accurate as any topographer's, but it was a lunar town, pure moonshine. He took extraordinary care to bring this false-truth alive. It was the same with people and scenery. Everything was described with the utmost attention to detail.

I read the letters and was moved. Maybe—it is possible—we were too weak for him. Around midnight a fierce warm wind played around the house; I got out of bed and closed the windows. I would not want to excuse my feminine frailty, I have no time for it, really, but that midnight I stood in front of the long mirror that used to hang above my mother's dressing table and took good stock of myself. I knew I was not yet old. By some peculiar whim of fate I had not aged much in twenty years: the years had left few marks on me. I was never plain, but mine was never the sort of beauty to which men seem to be drawn. It was respect and a kind of timid languishing that I inspired in them. Thanks to gardening and possibly my own metabolism I had not put on weight: I was tall, straight, and well proportioned. I had a few gray hairs now, but they were imperceptible among the light blond of the rest, my most characteristic feature. Time had drawn a few very delicate lines round my eyes and mouth, nor were my hands as they had been, having grown a little rough with housework. Nevertheless, when I looked in the mirror, I saw a woman waiting for her lover. It was, of course, a ridiculous momentary idea. I had passed forty-five. Lajos had long been living with someone else, he might even be married. I hadn't heard anything from him for years. Occasionally I saw his name in the papers, once with regard to some political scandal. It would not have surprised me if one day Lajos had become famous, or, indeed infamous. But the scandal quickly died away. Another time I read that he had fought a duel with someone in the courtyard of some barracks, had fired into the air and was uninjured! And this was all very much in keeping with his character, both the duel and the being uninjured. I have no idea whether he has ever been seriously ill, either. His fate lay elsewhere, I thought. And I got back into bed, together with my letters and memories and the sour-sweet consciousness of my lost youth.

I would be lying if I claimed to have felt particularly unfortunate in those hours. Oh yes, there was a time some twenty or twenty-two years ago when I was unfortunate. But the feeling gradually melted away, the wound scabbed over. It was an unfamiliar strength that enabled me to suppress the upwelling of pain. There are wounds time does not heal. I knew that I myself was not healed. Only a few years after our "separation"—it is very difficult to find the right word for what happened between Lajos and me—the unbearable suddenly became natural, simple. I no longer needed anything; I didn't need help, there was no need to call the police or the doctor or the priest. Somehow or other I continued living . . . Eventually there was a circle of friends, people who assured me that they needed me. A couple of them even proposed: Tibor, who was some years younger, and Endre, whom only Nunu addresses in the deferential way, as "Mister Endre," though he is not a day older than Lajos. Somehow or other I managed this game or accident quite well. The suitors remained good friends. That night I also reflected how life, in some miraculous fashion, had been kinder to me than I could ever have hoped.

4

*I*t was after midnight that Nunu came into my room. Our house still has no electric light—Mama had no time for the invention, and after her death we kept postponing it because of the expense—so Nunu's entrances tend to be a little theatrical. This time, too, she stood there with the flickering candle in her hand, her gray hair standing up everywhere, in her nightgown, like some midnight apparition. "Lady Macbeth," I said, smiling. "Come over here and sit down." I knew she would look in on me that night.

Nunu is the family member who "stands in" for all the other family members in the house. She had arrived thirty years before, part of the nomadic process whereby families drift about the world like mythical figures: she arrived out of an archaic past, part of the genealogical fabric of great-aunts and grandnieces, just for a few weeks. Then she stayed because she was needed. And later she stayed because everyone else in the family had died off before her, so Nunu was left, decade on decade, step by step, to ascend the ladder of family hierarchy, until she finally took Grandmother's place, moved into the room upstairs, and inherited her sphere of influence. Then Mama died, and then Vilma. One day Nunu noticed that she was not "standing in" for anybody; she noticed that she, the newcomer—she, the remnant—was the only family.

The successful conclusion of this complex career did not go to her head. Nunu had no ambition to be "mother" to me, nor did she pretend to be a guardian angel. As years went by she became ever more taciturn and sensible, so ruthlessly and dryly sensible it seemed she must have experienced everything life had to offer, so matter-of-fact and impassive she might have been a piece of furniture. Laci once said that Nunu had the air of something varnished, like an old walnut cabinet. She always dressed the same, summer and winter, in a dress of some smooth material that was not silk but was not taffeta either and which struck strangers, and even me, as a little too Sunday-best. In recent years she spoke just as much as was necessary and no more. She never told me anything of her previous life. I knew she wanted to share my every thought, my every care, but this plea was silent, and when she did say something it was as if we had been arguing for months, arguing fiercely and passionately, about the same subject, and she were simply putting the final full stop to it with a brief sentence. This was the way she spoke now as she sat down on my bed.

"Have you had the ring looked at?"

I sat up and rubbed my temples. I knew what she was thinking; I also knew that she was right: we had never talked about this, in fact I may never have showed her the ring, but still I knew she would be right, that the ring would prove a fake. I guessed as much. Nunu was uncanny like this. When did she hear of the ring? I wondered, then put the question aside, because it was perfectly natural that Nunu should know everything that pertained to the house, to the family, to my person, indeed to my life, including everything my dead sister had hidden away in the cellar or in the attic, so she would have known of the ring too. I had all but forgotten the story of the ring, because it was painful to think of it. When Vilma died, Lajos gave me this piece of jewelry, Grandmama's ring. This middling-size diamond set in platinum was the only object of value my family possessed. I can't quite understand how it remained in our possession—Father, too, valued the ring, regarding it with superstitious awe, and took great care of it though he was free enough with land and other valuables. It had the status of those famous diamonds in royal collections, the Kohinoor, the kind of precious stones that go in catalogs, whose market value no one considers and which are only meant to sparkle at the official anniversaries of dynasties, on the finger of a leading member of the family or on a queen's brow, and that was how we, four generations of us, had guarded it, "the ring." I never knew the actual value of the stone. In any case it would have fetched a good price, though nothing as princely as family legend would have it. It passed from Grandmama to Mama, and after our mother's death it went to Vilma. When Vilma died Lajos suddenly waxed sentimental and in a moment of high pathos presented it to me.

I well remember the scene. Vilma had been buried in the afternoon. When we returned from the funeral I lay down exhausted on the divan in my darkened room. Lajos entered, head to foot in black, having dressed with such care for the funeral he might have been a soldier on parade—I recall he had special black buttons made for the occasion—and with a few grave words he handed me the ring. I was so tired and confused that I didn't properly understand what he said and just stared vacantly as he placed the ring on the little table beside the divan, nor did I object when later he reminded me of the ring and put it on my finger. "You should have the ring," he solemnly declared. I came to my senses afterward. The ring belonged to Éva, naturally: it belonged to my dead sister's daughter, of course it did. But Lajos found an ingenious way to counter my argument. This kind of ring, he said, is not a family heirloom, it is a symbol, the symbol of family hierarchy. It therefore followed that after the deaths of both Mother and Vilma it should pass to me, since I was the oldest female. That settled it.

I said nothing and put the ring away. I had no intention, of course, not for a moment, of keeping the family heirloom. My conscience and the letter I have written in the case of my death—it's there in the sideboard next to the ring and the underwear—bears witness to the fact that I have kept it for Éva and have arranged for her to have it when I die. Then I decided to send the ring to Vilma's daughter for her engagement or her wedding, should she marry. The letter that deals with my few humble possessions clearly appoints Vilma's orphans as the inheritors, on condition that they should not sell the house or the garden while Nunu is alive. (Somehow I imagined Nunu would go on living for many years yet, and why not? She has no particular reason to die, just as she has no particular reason to live! In any case the feeling that she will outlive me is both exciting and reassuring.) I put the ring away because I didn't want to argue with Lajos and because I felt that this modest piece of jewelry, which might nevertheless help one of us given our circumstances—I thought the price it would fetch might cover the cost of a young woman's trousseau—was better placed with me than be lost in the kind of clutter that naturally accumulated around Lajos, clutter that multiplied like weeds in a favorable climate. He'll sell it or lose it in a game of cards, I thought, and was somewhat moved by his gesture of offering it to me. And just at the moment—God give me strength and help me be honest—when we had just laid my sister's coffin in the earth, I hoped that the lives of Lajos, the children, and, indeed, my own life, might be put in order. The ring no longer mattered very much, it was the situation as a whole that mattered . . . So I put the ring away. And that's how I took it away with me later when we separated and hid it among my mementos together with my will.

And in the meantime, in those years when I saw nothing of Lajos, I did not once look at the ring, because I was certain, the way a sleepwalker is certain, that the ring was fake.

"I was certain." What a thing to say! I had never held the ring in my hands. I was frightened of it. I feared the knowledge I had never put into words. I couldn't help but know that everything Lajos touched lost its original meaning and value, broke down into its elements, changed as did the noble metals once the alchemists got them into their retorts . . . I couldn't help but know that Lajos was not only capable of changing the nature of metals and stones but could turn true people into false ones. I couldn't help but know that a ring could not remain an innocent object once Lajos got his hands on it. Vilma had been ill a long time and couldn't mind all the household affairs, so Lajos had the run of the place and had taken possession of the ring . . . the very moment Nunu said it, I knew it was true. Lajos had conned me with the ring, as with everything else. I sat up in bed, quite pale.

"Have you had a look at it?"

"Yes," said Nunu quite calmly. "One time when you were not at home and left me with the keys. I took it to the jeweler. He had changed the setting too. He had picked some white metal for the clasp. Steel is less valuable than platinum. White gold, they said. He had changed the stone too. The ring you have looked after so carefully all these years is not worth five *krajcárs*."

"That's not true," I said.

Nunu shrugged.

"Wake up, Esther!" she scolded me.

I watched the candle flame and said nothing. Of course, if Nunu said it, it must be true. And why should I pretend not to have suspected it for a long time, from the moment Lajos gave me the ring. A fake, I thought there and then. Everything he touches instantly becomes a fake. And his breath, it's like the plague, I thought. I clenched my hand into a fist. It wasn't because of the ring . . . what did a ring or any number of rings matter at my time of life? Everything he has touched is fake, I thought. And then I thought something else, saying it out loud:

"Was giving it to me a calculated act? Because he feared being pursued, by the children or someone else, later . . . and since the ring was a fake anyway he gave me the copy so they should discover I had it and once it turned out to be fake, blame me?"

I was thinking aloud, as I always did when with Nunu. If anyone understood Lajos it was old Nunu, who knew him inside and out and read his every thought, even those thoughts he dared not actually think. Nunu was always fair. She answered in her usual way, gently and without fuss.

"I don't know. It's possible. But that would be a really lowdown thing to do. Lajos was not a schemer of that kind. Lajos has never once committed a criminal act. And he loved you. I don't think he would have used the ring to drag your name through the dirt. It simply happened that he had to sell the ring because he needed the money, but lacked the courage to admit he had sold it. So he had a copy made. And he gave you that worthless copy. Why? Was it a calculated act? Was it cheating? Maybe he just wanted to be generous. It was such a wonderful moment, everyone arriving fresh from Vilma's funeral, his first gesture being to hand over to you the family's only valuable heirloom. I suspected it as soon as you described the grand moment. That's why I had it looked at later. It's a fake."

"Fake," she repeated mechanically, in the flattest of tones.

"Why wait to tell me now?" I asked her.

Nunu brushed a few gray locks from her forehead.

"There was no need to tell you everything straightaway," she said, almost tenderly. "You had had quite enough bad news about Lajos."

I got out of bed, went over to the sideboard, and searched out the ring in the secret drawer, Nunu helping me look in the light of the billowing candle flame. Having found it, I held the ring to the flame and thoroughly examined it. I don't know anything about precious stones.

"Scratch the surface of the mirror with it," suggested Nunu.

But the stone made no mark on the glass. I put on the ring and gazed at it. The stone sparkled with a cold vacant light. It was a perfect copy, created by a master.

We remained sitting on the edge of the bed gazing at the ring. Then Nunu kissed me, gave a sigh, and went off without a word. I carried on sitting there for a long time staring at the fake stone. Lajos has not even arrived yet, I thought, but he has already taken something from me. That's all he can do, it seems. That's the way it is, it is his constitution. A terrible constitution, I thought, and started shivering. That's how I fell asleep, all goose-flesh, the fake ring on my finger, my senses dulled. I was like someone who has spent too long in a stuffy room then suddenly feels dizzy in the pitiless sharp air of truth that roars about her like a gale.

5

$\mathcal{T}$he day Lajos returned to us happened to fall on a
Sunday at the end of September. It was a wonder-
fully mild day, its colors glassy and clear. Gossamer was
drifting between the trees, and the air was sparklingly
clear without a trace of mist, a thin transparent solution
coating everything with the finest enamel, as if all visi-
ble objects, including the sky itself, had been touched in
with the most delicate of brushes. I went out into the
garden in the early morning and cut three dahlias for
the vase. Our garden is not particularly big, but it does
completely surround the house. I don't think it had
passed eight o'clock yet. I was standing in the dew, in
the great silence, when I heard conversation on the
veranda. I recognized the voices of my brother and
Tibor. They were talking quietly, and in the stillness of

the morning every word rang out as clear as if it had been broadcast by some invisible loudspeaker.

In the first few moments I would like to have intervened and warned them that I could hear it all, that they were not alone. But already the first sentence, spoken in a low voice, silenced me. Laci, my brother, was asking:

"Why didn't you marry Esther?"

"Because she wouldn't have me," came the answer.

I knew Tibor's voice, and my heart beat loud in my chest. Yes, this was Tibor, his quiet, calm voice, and every word of his was the kindly, slightly melancholy truth spoken patiently and dispassionately.

Why does Laci ask such things? I thought, insulted and agitated. My brother's questions always have an air of accusation: they sound aggressive and unbearably intimate. Laci hates any kind of secret. But people like their secrets. Might another man have given an evasive answer and protested against this invasion of privacy? Tibor answered quietly, as honest and correct as if someone had asked him a question about the railway timetable.

"Why wouldn't she have you?" my brother badgered him.

"Because she loved someone else."

"Who?" came the flat, ruthless question.

"Lajos."

Then they fell silent. I heard the scrape of a match, one of them lighting a cigarette. It was so quiet I even heard Tibor blow the match out. The question I was anticipating came as perfectly on cue as thunder after lightning. Laci was doing the asking.

"Do you know he is coming here today?"

"I know."

"What does he want?"

"I don't know."

"Does he owe you money too?"

"Let it go," a reluctant voice replied. "It was a long time ago. It doesn't matter anymore."

"He owes me," Laci declared with childish pride, as if it were something to boast about. "He had borrowed Father's gold watch too. He asked me to lend it to him for a week. That was ten years ago. No, wait, twelve years. He still hasn't given it back. Another time he took away the complete set of encyclopedias. Borrowed. I never saw those encyclopedias again. He asked me for three hundred korona. But I didn't give him that," said the voice, with the same childish self-satisfaction.

And the other voice, the deeper, quieter, more even one, answered rather modestly.

"It wouldn't have been such a disaster if you had given it to him."

"You think so?" Laci asked, suddenly ashamed. I stood among the flowerbeds and could almost see the blush on that aged child-face of his as he smiled in confusion. "What do you think? Does he still love Esther?"

There was a long wait before he received an answer to this. I really would like to have said something myself, but it was too late. It was a ridiculous situation. Here I was, alone, much older, surrounded by the flowers in my garden like the heroine of some old-fashioned poem, on the very morning when I was waiting for him to call, the man who had deceived and robbed me, here in the very house where it had all happened and where I had spent my entire life, where I kept Vilma and Lajos's letters in a sideboard along with the ring that I knew for certain, at least since the previous night—though I had previously suspected it—was fake, theatrically overhearing a theatrical conversation, waiting for an answer to a question, the only question of any interest to me, and what happens? The answer is delayed. Tibor, the conscientious judge of the situation, weighed his words carefully.

"I don't know," he said after a time. "I don't know," he repeated more quietly, as if arguing with someone. "Doomed love cannot die," he finally added.

Then they said more in low voices and went into the house. I could still hear them, looking for me. I put the flowers down on the concrete bench and walked to the bottom of the garden, to the well, and sat down on the bench where Lajos had proposed to me twenty-two years before. There I crossed my arms above my heart, drew the crocheted scarf over my breasts because I was cold, looked out at the highway, and suddenly could not understand Laci's question.

6

When Lajos first appeared among us, which seems a very long time ago, Laci was effusive in his welcome. Both were rehearsing the family role of "men of great promise." Nobody could say what exactly it was that Lajos and Laci "promised," though if you listened long enough to either of them both would have promised a great deal. The resemblance between their characters—the complete lack of any sense of reality, the tendency to unproductive dreaming, a compulsion to tell unconscious lies—drove them together with such irresistible force they might have been lovers. How proud Laci was when he introduced Lajos to the family! They even looked like each other: both their faces radiated something of the last century's romantic glow, a quality I liked in Laci and that helped me warm to

Lajos. There was a time when they dressed like each other, and the town was full of stories of their frivolous, grand-sounding antics. But everyone forgave them because they were young and charming and hadn't actually done anything scandalous. They were frighteningly alike in both soul and body.

This friendship, which even in their university years had an unsettling air of intimacy, did not cease when Lajos started showing interest in me: it did not cease but rather changed in an odd way. Even a blind man could see that Laci was ridiculously possessive of Lajos, doing everything he possibly could to make his friend part of the family while at the same time disapproving of Lajos's courtship, interrupting our clumsy moments of togetherness, mocking the uncertain signs of our increasing mutual attraction. Laci was possessive, but in an extraordinary—or perhaps not so extraordinary—way he directed his jealousy only at me and appeared to be happy when Lajos married Vilma, behaving throughout with the utmost tenderness toward them, prepared to sacrifice anything for their happiness. Everyone in the family knew that I was Laci's favorite, the one for whom he had a fond spot. Later I even thought that Laci's opposition and antagonism might have played some part in Lajos's infidelity. But this wasn't a hypothesis I could ever prove, even to myself.

These two similar people, these two almost identical characters, rivaled each other in friendship. Once Lajos came into his inheritance they even lived together in the capital, in a magnificent bachelor apartment that I never visited but which, according to Laci, was one of the most significant intellectual and social venues of the age. I have every reason to doubt its social significance. In any case, they lived together and had money—Lajos was pretty close to being a rich man at the time, and it was only a childish resentment in Laci that made him mention the gold watch and the few hundred Lajos had wanted to borrow, since Lajos, in the days of his wealth, was generous to everyone, including, of course, his closest friend. They selected a few happily idle members of the *jeunesse d'orée* and lived a life of high jinks. Not that there were debaucheries as such. Lajos, for example, was not particularly fond of wine, and Laci was no night hawk. No, their lives were complex, expensive, and given over to an exacting kind of idleness, the kind of idleness an ignorant outsider might easily mistake for substantial, deliberate activity, amounting to a refined form of life fashionably referred to as "lifestyle"—Laci's favorite word. These two peculiarly talented young men strove to realize it together. The reality was that they were lying and dreaming. But I only discovered that much later.

With Lajos, the new friend, a whole new set of tensions entered our household. He looked on our rural amusements and lives with a certain bemused condescension. We sensed his superiority and, a little abashed, strove to overcome our shortcomings. We all suddenly started "reading," particularly authors to whose significance Lajos first drew our attention—"reading" with such industriousness, with such a sense of shame, it was as if we were preparing for the most important examination life could offer. Later we discovered that Lajos himself had never read, or had simply scanned, these authors and thinkers, the works and ideas that he so emphatically recommended, wagging his head and chiding us with good-humored severity. His charm acted on us like a cheap wicked spell. Our poor mother was the first to be utterly bedazzled. Under Lajos's influence and out of deference to him we "read" all the time, quite differently from before, and also tried to live "a social life," but one quite different from before. We even refurbished the place. It cost a lot of money, and we were not rich. Mother was always waiting for Lajos, preparing for his visits as if for some kind of test. One time she was mugging up on the latest German philosophers, because Lajos, in his superior way, had asked whether we were acquainted with the works of B, the Heidelberg thinker. No, of course we weren't. We urgently started reading his high and somewhat cloudy meditations on life and death. Father too was pulling himself together. He drank less and was particularly careful when we had guests to hide his sad patchwork life from Lajos's all-seeing eye. Every weekend my brother and Lajos would arrive with guests.

The house would be full of people and chatter then. The old parlor had been transformed into some kind of "salon" where Lajos entertained the most fascinating local people, people who had until that time been not so much fascinating as suspicious, people we would not have had in the house at all. Suddenly they had an open invitation. In his worn frock-coat, and with old-fashioned cordiality, my father moved awkwardly among the weekend guests—he dared not even light his pipe on these occasions . . . And Lajos accepted me, tested me, approved or admonished me with a glance, praised me to the skies and rewarded me or cast me headlong into hell. This lasted three years.

My brother and his strange friend were not vulgar, dissolute young men in the ordinary sense of the word. After a year everyone noticed that Laci had become as dependent on Lajos as we all had, my mother, Vilma, and, later, myself. I could claim now to have been the only sensible one, the sole figure immune to this wicked illusion, but why should I console myself with such a poor distinction? Yes, I did "see through" Lajos straight-away, but did I not rush blindly and eagerly to serve him? He was so solemn and so sensitive. We were quickly forced to acknowledge that he and Laci had abandoned their academic studies. One day at dusk he was standing by the table with a lock of hair flopping over his forehead when he said—and I remember his words exactly, words he pronounced resignedly, as if performing an act of self-sacrifice—"I must exchange the quiet and lonely existence of the study for the noisy, dangerous battlefield of life." He always spoke as if reading from a book. This declaration shook me and upset me. I felt that Lajos was abandoning his vocation for some great, somewhat obscure project in order to enter a struggle on behalf of somebody or for a whole lot of somebodies, in which he should be armed not with the weapons of knowledge but with those of guile and pragmatism. The sacrifice made me uneasy, because in our family we preferred boys to complete their edu-cation before entering "the battlefield of life." But I believed Lajos when he said his way was different, his weapons not the usual kind. Naturally enough, Laci immediately followed him on his chosen path; they did not bother with the third year of their university course. I was still quite a young girl then. Laci returned to the "world of the mind" some time later; using the last remaining part of our family's credit he opened a book-shop in town and after all the enthusiasm of the planning stage filled his life with the selling of textbooks and stationery. Lajos was severely critical of this turn in his career, but later, when politics became our passion, he kept his peace.

I never got to know Lajos's political views. Tibor, whom I often consulted on this kind of issue, shrugged and said Lajos had no political convictions at all, that he sailed with the prevailing wind and simply wanted to be involved wherever power was being distributed. It might have been fair criticism, and yet it wasn't quite accurate enough. I suspected Lajos was just as liable to make sacrifices for humankind or human ideals—especially the latter, since he always preferred ideas to reality, probably because the field of ideas was likely to prove less dangerous and it was easier compromising with them—and when he sought "involvement" in politics he was willing to put himself on the line, not so much for the prizes available, but for the sheer excitement of being involved, the pathos of involvement being something he fully felt and suffered. My experience of Lajos is that he is the kind of man who begins with lies but then in the middle of his lying grows passionate and weeps, going on to lie more, this time with tears in his eyes, until eventually, to everyone's utter surprise, he tells the truth as eloquently as he had been telling the opposite . . . This talent of his naturally did not prevent him from presenting himself for a whole decade as a vanguard proponent of extreme and conflicting views, and he was soon shown the door by all parties. Fortunately Laci did not follow him on this path. He remained in "the intellectual realm," selling drawing material and dog-eared secondhand textbooks, part of that faintly musty atmosphere. But Lajos went in search of danger, "dangers" he could never quite pin down, leaving us to contemplate him at a distance, a lone figure surviving among storms and tempests, never too far from where lightning was liable to strike.

When Vilma died and the family broke up, Lajos vanished from our horizon. That was when I returned here, to this humble place of last refuge. Nothing awaited me here, it was only somewhere to lay my head and a few dry crumbs. But for anyone who has been through a storm, any shelter is welcome.

7

This shelter—or that's what it seemed to be at the beginning—was more than a little shaky. When Father died, the executors, Tibor and Endre, made a thorough examination of the estate. Endre, the public notary, was constrained to do so by virtue of his office. Our financial position seemed impossible at first. The little that remained after the latest upheavals—my father's resentful neglect and ill-tempered dealings, Mama's illness, Vilma's dispossession and death, the capital required by Laci to establish his business—all drained away to Lajos by way of narrow, invisible channels. Once he could no longer lay hands on money he started removing objects from the old house, as "mementos," he said, combining the curiosity of a child with the avidity of a collector. Later I would sometimes defend him against Endre and Tibor's criticism. "He's only playing," I said when they charged him with rapacity. "There is something childish in his makeup. He likes to play." Endre sharply disagreed. Children played with model boats or colored marbles, he indignantly argued; Lajos was the kind of "eternal child" who preferred to play with bank bills. He did not say, though you could pick up the hint, that these bills, Lajos's bills, were not to be regarded as entirely pure and harmless playthings. And indeed, after Father's death some bills turned up that Father appeared to have signed over to Lajos, though I myself never questioned their validity. Then these too leaked away, as did everything else, in the general collapse.

When I noticed that I had no one left in the world—except Nunu, with whom I lived in a certain interdependent relationship, as mistletoe to tree, though neither of us knew which was the tree and which the parasite—Endre and Tibor endeavored to save something for me out of the wreckage. This was the time when Tibor wanted me to marry him. I hemmed and hawed but couldn't give him the real reason for my rejection. I couldn't tell him that in my heart of hearts I was still waiting for Lajos, expecting news of some kind, a message, possibly some miracle. Anything to do with Lajos was charged with an air of miracle, so I did not think it in the least impossible that he should appear one day, somewhat theatrically perhaps, like Lohengrin, singing an exalted aria. But then, after our separation, he disappeared as miraculously as if he had wrapped himself in a cloak of invisibility. I heard nothing from him for years.

There was just the house and the garden now. There was also the question of some minor debt. I have always believed myself to be an inexhaustible, obstinate, practical being. But the moment I was left alone I was obliged to notice that I had been living in Cloud Cuckoo Land before—clouds heavy with thunder, I should add—and had hardly any idea of what was real and reliable and what was not. Nunu told me the garden and the house would be enough for the two of us. Even today I don't understand how it could be "enough." Certainly the garden is large and full of fruit trees and Nunu had banished those lush, decorative flowerbeds, the winding paths sprinkled with red clay, the romantic waterfall with its moss-covered rocks, intensely cultivating every inch of ground like one of those southern mountain dwellers who exploit their fields and gardens to the fullest, squaring off each square meter of plot with stone walls to protect them from storms and unwelcome visitors. The garden was all that was left. Endre and Tibor suggested we should let out some of the rooms and take in lodgers. The idea foundered primarily because of Nunu's opposition. She didn't say why she was against it, she offered no explanation, you could just tell from the tone of her voice and even more from her silences that she was not happy with having strangers in the house. Nunu always arranges things and "solves problems" in ways that you would not expect of her. Two lonely women with nothing to do might, or so the world thinks, set up as seamstresses or cooks, or advertise fancy embroidery, but Nunu did not consider any of these. It took some time before she allowed me to take on some of the neighbors' children for piano lessons.

We survived somehow . . . I know now it was the house that kept us going, that and the garden, all that our poor risk-taking father had left us. This was all that remained, all that sustained us. The house offered us shelter; even as it was, deprived of the old furniture, it provided a home. The garden provided food, just enough and no more than a castaway requires. Somehow it grew around us because we gave it all we had, feeding it with our labor and our hopes, so that sometimes it seemed like a proper estate where anyone who chose to tie himself to it could live without a thought. One day Nunu decided to take the end of the garden, the sandy part, a whole two acres, and plant it with almond trees. These almond trees were like mysterious hands that reached over us to shelter us, casting their almonds before the starving. Every year they brought good produce that Nunu managed, in her own secretive way, quite ceremonially, to put a price on, and it was from that sale that we managed to live, and, indeed, clear our debts, sometimes even to the extent of being able to help Laci. For a long time I did not understand how this was done. Nunu only smiled and kept her counsel. Sometimes I stopped in front of our small forest of almonds and stared at them as if superstitious. It was like a miracle there in the sand, in our lives. Someone is looking after us, I felt.

The almond orchard was Father's idea originally, but he was too tired by the end to make it happen. Once, some ten years ago, he had said to Nunu that the sandy back of the garden would be good for almonds. Father didn't much concern himself with what life had to offer; in the eyes of strangers it was he who had wasted the modest resources of our family. Even so, after his death we noticed that in his own silent, resentful way, he had left everything that was due to us in order; it was Mama who was the chief burden on the house; it was he who, by Lajos's request, kept the garden for our use, who argued to the last against moving away. When Nunu and I remained alone we had no more to do than take our place among the gardens that Father had made for us. We had the house renovated, thanks to Endre, who arranged a cheap loan against the bequest. All this happened without being planned: it simply happened without any particular intention or aim. One day we noticed we had a shelter over our heads. Occasionally I could buy material with which to make clothes, Laci could borrow what books were necessary, and the state of solitude we entered with such trepidation after the collapse, like wounded animals entering a cave, slowly dissolved around us, so soon we had friends and the house rang on Sundays with hearty male conversation. People looked after us, giving Nunu and me a place in the world, allocating us a slot in the nook of their imaginations where we could quietly get on with our lives. Life was nowhere near as unbearable or hopeless as I had imagined it would be. Slowly our lives were given over to new activities: we had friends and even a few enemies, such as Tibor's mother and Endre's wife, who, ridiculously and entirely without cause, resented their menfolk visiting our house. There were times when life in the house and the garden was like real life that has a purpose, a project, some inner meaning. It was just that it had no meaning; we could have gone on for years on end just as we were, but if someone had ordered us to leave the very next day I would have put up no resistance. Life was simple and safe. Lajos was a disciple of Nietzsche, who demanded that one should live dangerously, but he was frightened of danger, and when he entered into some political "involvement" he did so as he embarked on any passion, with a loud mouth and equipped with some "secret weapon," protecting himself with carefully calculated lies, with warm underwear, with some cosmetic items and the well-preserved, more scandalous letters of his adversaries in his pocket. But there was a time when I was close to him when my life was as "dangerous" as his. Now that this danger has passed I can see that nothing is as it was, and that such danger was in fact the one true meaning of life.

8

I went into the house, arranged the dahlias in vases, and sat down with my guests on the veranda. Every Sunday morning Laci escapes to us for breakfast. At that time we lay the table for him, especially on the veranda or, if the weather is bad, in the old nursery, which we now use as a parlor. We put out the old cups and the English cutlery, and he pours cream from the silver jug he received as a christening present fifty-two years ago from a do-gooding relative with modest tastes. My brother's name is engraved in italics on it. They were sitting on the veranda, Tibor puffing at a cigar, looking at the garden with concern, Laci eating with his mouth full as he had done in his adolescence. He was loath to miss these Sunday breakfasts. They seemed to conjure the precise details of his childhood for him.

"He has written to Endre too," said Laci, full-mouthed.

"What did he write?" I asked, and went pale.

"He wrote that he should be available, that he shouldn't be traveling anywhere that day. That he needed him."

"Needed Endre?" I asked, laughing out loud.

"Tibor, it's true, isn't it?" asked Laci, because he always had to have a reliable witness. Laci dared not trust his own pronouncements now.

"Yes, it's true," said Tibor impatiently. "He wants something. Perhaps," and his face brightened here, as if he had found the one proper and honorable solution to a problem, "perhaps he wants to settle his debts."

We thought about that. I wanted to believe in Lajos, and now that Tibor had put forward this theory I myself did not feel it to be impossible. A flood of wild joy and sincere conviction rushed through me. Well, of course! After twenty years he wants to come home. He is coming here, where—and why should we pussyfoot around the issue?—he was indebted to everyone in some way, with money, with promises, with oaths! He is returning to a place where every meeting is bound to be fraught and painful for him; he is coming back to face the past, to keep his word at last! What strength, what hope, suffused my entire being at that moment! I was no longer afraid of meeting him again. People tend not to return, not after a decade of absence, to the places where they have failed. It must have taken him a long time to prepare himself for this difficult journey, I thought sympathetically. He will have prepared for a long time and who knows what false trails he had explored, what precipices he had avoided to arrive at this decision? It was as though I had suddenly awoken. This foolish hope that had chased away every sensible scruple, this clarity that was as brilliant as the rising of the sun, that now took hold of me in anticipation of Lajos's arrival, completely vanquished all my doubts. Lajos was coming with the children, he was already on his way, he was quite close to me right then. And we who knew him, we who knew his weaknesses, must prepare for the great reckoning when Lajos would render everyone their due: he would fulfil his oaths, pay off his debts! Nunu, who had appeared silently at the door with hands linked under her knitted shawl, listened to our conversation and quietly intervened.

"Endre has sent to say he will be here in a moment. He says Lajos asked him to attend in an official capacity."

The message only served to raise my hopes still higher. Lajos required a notary! We were talking wildly. Laci announced that the whole town had heard about Lajos's impending arrival. Last night in the café a tailor had come up to Laci and started talking about Lajos's old unsettled bills. A town councillor mentioned the concrete benches he had ordered some fifteen years ago on Lajos's urging, benches on which a deposit had been paid but had never arrived. This gossip no longer troubled my memories. Lajos's past was compounded of such easy-come, easy-go schemes and promises. Now they seemed merely acts of childish irresponsibility. We had been through some difficult times since then. Lajos had passed fifty and no longer told fibs. He would take responsibility for what he had done and was already on his way to us. I left the company to put on some decent clothes appropriate for such a ceremonial occasion. Laci was reminiscing.

"He was always asking for something. Do you remember, Tibor, the last time you saw him after that great argument when you told him to his face that he was a scoundrel, and you enumerated his faults, all the harm he had done his family and friends, and said he was the lowest of the low; how he cried and then embraced everyone and as a farewell gesture asked you for more money? A hundred or two hundred? Do you remember? . . ."

"I don't remember," said Tibor, ashamed and uncomfortable.

"But you must!" cried Laci. "And when you refused to give it to him, he rushed off, in a state, like someone about to meet his death. We were right here then, in this very garden, just ten years younger, thinking about Lajos. But he stopped at the gate, returned and quite quietly and calmly asked you for twenty, 'or at least some change' as he put it—because he hadn't enough money for the train! And then you did give him the money. Was there ever such a man!" Laci passionately declared, and carried on eating.

"Yes, I gave it to him," Tibor admitted with embarrassment. "Why wouldn't I have given it to him? I could never understand why people should not give money if they had it. And that wasn't the main thing with Lajos," he said pensively, gazing at the ceiling with nearsighted eyes.

"Money was not important to Lajos?" asked Laci, genuinely astonished. "That's like saying blood is of no interest to wolves."

"You don't understand," said Tibor, reddening. He always reddened when there was a conflict with his role as a magistrate, the role that calls for guardedness and judgment, where he had to give the right verdict knowing that this verdict did not accord with the general sense of justice in which most people believed, and which he had sworn to uphold. "You don't understand," he repeated obstinately. "I have thought a great deal about Lajos. It's all a question of motive. Lajos's motives were entirely honorable. I can think of one occasion . . .

at some party when he asked for money, quite a lot of money, and the next morning I discovered that he had given the whole lot to one of my clerks who had gotten into trouble. Wait, I haven't finished. It's not a heroic act of self-sacrifice, of course, being a philanthropist with someone else's money. But Lajos too had urgent need of cash, his bills had expired, what shall I say . . . they were unpleasant bills. And this amount that he borrowed, drunk as he was, and that he handed over the next morning, sober, to a stranger, would have helped him too. Do you understand?"

"No," replied Laci, in all sincerity.

"I believe I do understand," said Tibor, and then as usual when regretting his words, fell stubbornly silent.

Nunu simply added, "Be careful, because it's money he's after. It will be useless being careful, of course. Tibor is bound to give him more."

"No, I'll not do that again," said Tibor, laughing and shaking his head.

Nunu shrugged. "Of course you won't! Like the last time. You'll give him something. Another twenty. He is a man to whom one must give."

"But why, Nunu?" asked Laci, utterly astonished and clearly jealous.

"Because he is stronger," said Nunu indifferently. Then she went back into the kitchen.

I was dressing, standing in front of the mirror, when

I felt dizzy and had to grope for support. I had a vision. I saw the past so clearly it seemed to be the present. I saw the garden, the same garden where we were just now waiting for Lajos, waiting under the great ash, but then we were twenty years younger, our hearts full of despair and anger. Harsh, passionate words buzzed like flies in the autumn air. It was autumn then too, toward the end of September. The air was scented and damp. We were twenty years younger then, relatives, friends, and vague acquaintances, and Lajos was standing in our midst like a thief caught red-handed. I see him there as he stands, unflummoxed, blinking a little, occasionally removing his glasses and carefully wiping them. He is alone at the center of the agitated circle, as calm as anyone can be when they know the game is up, that all is discovered and there is nothing left to do except stand patiently and listen while judgment is pronounced. Then suddenly he is gone, and we are living on in our mechanical way, like wax dolls. But it is as if we only appeared to be living; our true lives were the battles we had with Lajos, our passion the exasperation with him.

Now here he was about to be in the old circle, in the old garden. Now we would start to live again with the same passionate exasperation. I put on my lilac dress. It was like donning an old theatrical costume, the clothes of life. I felt that everything a man might stand for—his strength, his own particular way of life—roused in his adversaries a specific image of what it means to be alive. We all belonged to him, had combined against him, and now that he was on his way to us, we were living different lives, more exciting, more dangerous lives. I stood before the mirror in my room, in my old dress, feeling all this. Lajos was bringing back both the past and the timeless experience of being alive. I knew he had not changed. I knew Nunu would be right. I knew there was nothing we could do to defend ourselves. But at the same time I knew that I still had no clue about life, about my own life and the lives of others, and it was only through Lajos that I could learn the truth—yes, through the liar, Lajos. The garden was filling up with acquaintances. A car was sounding its horn somewhere. Suddenly I felt a great calm descend on me: I knew Lajos had come because he had no choice, and that we were welcoming him because we had no choice, and the whole thing was as terrifying, as unpleasant, and as unavoidable for him as it was for us.

9

*B*ut reality, that miraculous ice-cold shower, woke me from my dream. Lajos had arrived and the day had begun, the day of Lajos's visit, the day of which Tibor, Laci, and Endre would speak until their dying day, confusing his words, correcting each other, conjuring and refuting various images of the truth. I'd like to give a faithful representation of the events of that day. It took me some time to understand the true significance of his visit. It began like the publicity for a traveling circus. And it ended . . . but no, I can't compare the end, his departure, to anything. It ended so simply. Lajos left, the day ended, as did an episode of our lives. We carried on living.

Lajos arrived complete with menagerie. The car that stopped in front of the house had already aroused people's interest. It was red and conspicuously large, like some public conveyance. I missed the moment, the long-awaited moment of his arrival, and could only piece together from Laci's useless account, as carefully corrected by Tibor, how the first to emerge from the car was a peculiarly dressed young man with a yellow lion-headed dog in his arms. The dog was of some expensive Tibetan breed, angry and liable to bite. The young man was followed by an older woman with a painted face, whose outfit was more appropriate for someone younger, with a leather coat on top, then Éva, then Gábor, and, lastly, the figure sitting next to the driver, Lajos. Their arrival confused the welcoming party. No one hastened to greet them. They stood in the garden, stared at the red car, and did not move a muscle. Lajos was talking to the driver, then he entered the garden, looked around, recognized Tibor, and without even a hello said:

"Do you have a twenty, Tibor? The driver needs to buy some oil and I have no change."

And because he had chosen to say exactly what everyone was expecting him to say, no one protested or got annoyed: they were all under his spell, in the garden in which they had last seen him twenty years ago, under the same tree, in the same light, and because he addressed them in exactly the same words with which he had left them, they understood that this was part of an unalterable law and fell silent. Tibor numbly extended the requested banknote to him. They stood there a while longer like actors in a mime. Then Lajos paid the driver, returned to the garden, and introduced the newcomers to the company. That's how it began.

Later I often wondered whether it was something Lajos set up, something smacking of theater. I believe it was, it was just that the theatricality was unconscious. Lajos wouldn't have the effect he does if it were deliberate, since ordinary braggarts and amoral buffoons who provide some brief amusement or rouse fierce debate in their social circle grow tiresome eventually and find that people turn away from them, precisely because everything they do is calculated and predictable. But people don't turn away from Lajos, because his little shows are full of surprises that he himself enjoys but does not prepare, and when the punch line is delivered he loves nothing better than to laugh dreamily and applaud himself. Lajos would often recite the speech in Shakespeare that begins, "All the world's a stage . . ." He performed on that stage and always played the leading role in the historical present, never studying the part. Even now, in the very moment of his arrival, he was directing, presenting, and speechifying with transparent pleasure. He introduced his children with a gesture that was hard to classify but was unmistakably melodramatic, as though they were orphans.

His first words were accusing, accusing and pleading. Behold the orphans! he declared to Tibor and Laci, indicating the two children who had in the meantime grown up: Gábor, a shifty, sluggish, blinking, and overweight young man, now a qualified engineer; and Éva, a little madam, very much the lady-about-town in her modish sporting outfit, with two fox furs round her neck, and wearing a slightly mocking, resentful smile of anticipation. *Behold the orphans!* Lajos's gesture implied when introducing us to Vilma's children, who were indeed orphans, or rather half-orphans, who had by now overcome whatever difficulties fate had presented them with. They had grown up and returned to us out of the past in confidence-inspiring physical health. It is hard for me to explain this. We stood there confused, just as we were to do later, facing the orphans but averting our eyes. Lajos kept showing them off, from the front, from the side, as if he had found them on the street deserted by God and man like ragged urchins, as if someone in the house—Tibor or Nunu or possibly I myself—were responsible for the orphans' predicament. He did not blame us in so many words, but right from the beginning that was the manner in which he presented us with Éva and Gábor. And what was stranger still was that, looking at these two well-fed, apparently well-dressed, and, what was more, suspiciously mature, poised young people who had dropped out of the sky into our laps, we who were gathered in the garden actually felt responsible for everything, responsible in the common sense of the word, as though we had refused to share a crust or our affections with someone who had a right to expect such things and had need of them. The two orphans waited patiently, standing at ease, looking about as if they were used to Lajos's theatrical presentations, knowing there was nothing for it but to wait till the performance was over and the audience started applauding. After a carefully timed moment of silence, by which time our consciences were well and truly soaked in guilt regarding "the orphans," Lajos coughed twice, as he always used to do, then went into his conjuring act.

The magic show was to fill up the afternoon. He worked feverishly. It was clear this was going to be a bigger and better show than any before, the very acme of his art; his whole heart was in it, the tears were real, the kisses hot, and the feats of memory involved in compiling the various tricks were astonishing: his talent dazzled everyone. Even Nunu. In the first hour we could not get a word in. His performance left us breathless. He kissed Nunu twice, once on the right cheek, once on

the left, then took from his wallet a letter from the secretary of state, in which that high-ranking official
acknowledged the communication of his dear friend
Lajos, wherein he had urged the immediate appoint-
ment of Nunu as postmistress and was even now working on the case. I saw the letter with my own eyes; it was
on official paper, properly stamped and watermarked,
and the words "Secretary of State" appeared in the top
left-hand corner in a firm round hand. The letter was
genuine, the real thing. Lajos really had acted in Nunu's
interest. It was just that no one mentioned the fact that
he had promised Nunu to do this fifteen years ago, and
everyone kept silent about Nunu being almost seventy
years old now, about the fact that she had long given up
any ambition she had had of being a postmistress, was
no longer up to the task and could not be employed at
this age for such a position of responsibility, and that, in
short, Lajos's noble deed was precisely fifteen years too
late. No one gave this a thought. We stood round the
two of them, Lajos and Nunu, our eyes sparkling with
relief and exultation. Tibor looked round with pride,
his spectacles glinting with satisfaction. "There, you see.
We were wrong! Lajos has kept his promise after all,"
said the look. Laci smiled in confusion, but at that
moment he too was clearly proud of Lajos. Nunu wept.
Back home in the Felvidék she had been assistant post-

mistress for thirty years and vainly hoped to be pro-moted at last, but when this hope faded with the years she upped and moved to live with us and gave up her dreams of office. She read the letter now with tears in her eyes, deeply moved by the lines mentioning her by name; the secretary of state was not promising any-thing, but he said enough to hold out the hope that he would be well disposed in the matter of Nunu, and would "look into the possibility." None of this was of any practical use, but Nunu still wept and said quietly, "Thank you, Lajos darling. It's probably too late. But I am so happy."

"It's not too late," said Lajos. "You will see, it is not too late."

He declared this with such conviction it seemed he was on confidential terms not only with the secretary of state but with God himself, that he could arrange mat-ters of age and death too if he chose.

We heard him and were moved.

Then everyone fell to talking excitedly. "Mister" Endre arrived and stood beside the concrete bench a little reserved and confused, like someone whose appearance had not been entirely voluntary but had been summoned by Lajos in "an official capacity." Lajos was organizing things. He introduced people, arranged them into picturesque groups, and initiated little scenes—scenes of farewell, scenes of delight and tearful reconciliation—all this with a few words or a hint, concealing the true meaning and import of the meetings behind a facade of stagy artificial group compositions that were empty of content; and everyone played along, all of us smiling in confusion, even respectable Endre, with a briefcase under his arm, the contents of which we never discovered and which he must have brought with him for purely symbolic purposes, as a line of defense to show that he would not have come voluntarily but was on official business. And it was obvious that everyone was happy that Lajos was here, happy to be present at this reunion. I would not have been surprised to see a small crowd gather behind the garden palings and sing something. But the general confusion was so much like a deluge that individual details were lost in the flood of well-being. Later, about dusk, when we had recovered our senses, we stared at each other amazed, as if we had fallen under the spell of an Indian fakir at work; the fakir had thrown a rope into the air, climbed the rope, and disappeared among the clouds before our very eyes. We were looking at the sky, seeking him there, and were astonished to see that he was taking a bow among us, here on earth, his begging bowl in front of him.

10

Nunu had served a cooked breakfast, the guests had
settled down on the veranda, nervously eating and
getting to know one other. Everyone felt that it was only
the powerful spell of Lajos's presence that prevented loss
of temper. It was pure theater, every word of it. The
hours were artfully crammed: Scene One, "The meal,"
Scene Two, "A walk round the garden." Lajos, with his
director's eye, occasionally spotted this or that group
falling behind, and clapped his hands and brought the
company into line. At last he was alone with me in the
garden. Laci was on the veranda waxing enthusiastic,
rapt and unguarded, talking with his mouth full. It was
he who had first surrendered to Lajos's charm, forgot his
doubts, and was happily and openly bathing in the sun-
shine of the familiar presence. The first words Lajos

addressed to me were, "Now we have to put everything right."

Hearing this my heart began to beat loudly and nervously. I did not answer. I stood facing opposite him under the tree next to the concrete bench on which he had so often lied to me, and finally I took a good hard look at him.

There was something sad about him, something that reminded me of an aging photographer or politician who is not quite up-to-date regarding manners and ideas but continues obstinately, and somewhat resentfully, to employ the same terms of flattery he has used for years. He was an animal tamer past his prime, of whom the animals are no longer afraid. His clothes, too, were peculiarly old-fashioned: as if he were wanting to keep up with the fashions at all costs but some inner demon prevented him from being elegant or fashionable in the way he thought was necessary and which he liked. His tie, for example, was just a shade louder than was right for the rest of his outfit, his character and age, so he had the air of a gigolo. His suit was of a light color, fashionable in that it was loose and made for traveling, the kind you see movie moguls in magazines wear when they are globe-trotting. Everything was a little too new, specially chosen for the occasion, even his hat and shoes. And all this communicated a certain helplessness.

My heart went out to him. Perhaps, if he had come in rags, a broken man without a shred of hope, I would not have tolerated this cheap feeling of sympathy. He's had it coming to him, I would have thought. But this hopeless modishness, so redolent of shame, filled me with pity. I gazed at him and suddenly felt sorry for him.

"Sit down, Lajos," I said. "What do you want of me?"

I was calm and well meaning. I was no longer afraid of him. This man has known failure, I thought, and felt no satisfaction thinking that; in fact, I felt nothing but pity, a deep and humiliating pity. It was as if I had noticed that he was dyeing his hair or had committed something equally unbecoming; ideally I would have cursed him for the past and for the present, seriously cursed him, but without any particular severity. Suddenly I felt myself to be much older, much more mature than he was. Lajos had stopped developing at a certain point and had aged into an impudent, pedantic fraud, nothing particularly dangerous, indeed—and this was the sadder part—something rather aimless. His eyes were clear, gray, irresolute, as they had been so long ago when I last saw him. He smoked his cigarette through a long cigarette holder—his hands with their prominent veins had particularly aged, and never stopped trembling—and to top it all he was looking at me so attentively, so calmly and objectively, he clearly knew that for once it was pointless and in vain to try to deceive me; I knew his tricks, I knew the secrets of his art, and whatever he said in the end he would have to answer with or without words, but, this once, it would have to be the truth . . . Naturally, he began with a lie.

"I want to put everything right," he repeated mechanically.

"What do you want to put right?"

I looked into his eyes and laughed. Surely, this could no longer be serious! I thought. After a certain time has passed between people it is impossible to "put anything right"; I understood this hopeless truth the moment we were sitting together on the concrete bench. One lives and patches, improves, constructs, or, occasionally, ruins one's life, but after a while one notices that whatever has been so compounded of errors and accidents is quite unique. There was nothing more Lajos could do here. When somebody appears out of the past and announces in heartfelt tones that he wants to put "everything" right one can only pity his ambition and laugh at it: time has already "put things right" in its own peculiar way, the only way to put anything right. And so I answered:

"Forget it, Lajos. We are all happy, of course, to see you . . . the children and yourself. We don't know what you have in mind, but still we are happy to see you again. Let's not talk about the past. You don't owe anybody anything."

Even as I was speaking I noticed how I too was in the grip of the mood of the moment, I too was saying the first things that came into my head, things that were, to put it bluntly, lies. It was only an excess of feeling and the concomitant confusion that could have exaggerated and declared that the past no longer existed, that Lajos did not owe "anybody anything." We were both aware of this false note and gazed at the pebbles with downcast eyes. The tone we had adopted toward each other was pitched too high: too high, too dramatic, false. I suddenly noticed I had started to argue, not very logically but at least sincerely and with passion, since I could not hold myself back.

"I doubt whether that is the only reason you have come," I said quietly, because I feared that there on the veranda where the conversation occasionally fell silent people might be listening to us, hearing what I was saying.

"No," he said, and coughed. "No, that is not the only reason. No, Esther, I had to talk to you one last time."

"I have nothing left," I said involuntarily, somewhat daringly.

"I don't need anything anymore," he answered, evidently not insulted. "Now it is I who want to give you something. Look here, twenty years have passed, twenty years! There will not be many more twenty years like that now, these may be the last. In twenty years things become clearer, more transparent, more comprehensible. Now I know what happened, and even why it happened."

"How repulsive," I said, my voice breaking. "How repulsive and ridiculous. Here we sit on this bench, we who once mattered to each other, talking about the future. No, Lajos, there is no future of any kind, I mean for us. Let's get back to reality. There is something, a quality you are unaware of: it is a kind of modest dignity, the dignity of bare existence. I have been humiliated enough. Just talking about the past is humiliating. What do you want? What's the idea? Who are these strange people? One day you pack, round up some people and some animals, and arrive in the grand old manner, with the same old words, as if you were obeying a call from God . . . but people know you here. We know you, my friend."

I spoke calmly, with a certain ridiculous pomposity, pronouncing each word clearly and firmly as if I had been composing the speech for some time. The truth was I hadn't composed anything. Not for a moment did I believe that anything here could be "put right," I had no wish to fall into Lajos's arms, I didn't even want to argue with him. What did I want? I would like to have been indifferent. Here he is, he has arrived, this was just another episode in the peculiar pageant of life, he wants something, he's up to something, but then he'll go away and we will go on living as before. He no longer has any power over me! I felt and looked on him, safe, superior. He no longer has any power over me in the old sentimental sense. But at the same time I noticed that the excitement of this first conversation was far from indifference; the passion with which I spoke was a sign that there still existed a relationship that was far from fanciful, affected, or imagined, a relationship that was not mere moonshine, memory, or nostalgia. We were talking about something real. And, since it was vital, after so much mist and fog, to find a toehold in reality, I answered quickly without choosing my words.

"You have nothing to give me. You took everything, ruined everything."

He answered as I expected him to.

"That's true."

He looked at me with clear gray eyes, then stared straight in front of him. He pronounced the words childishly, with an air of wonder, as if someone had praised him for passing an exam. I shuddered. What kind of man was this? He was so calm. Now he was looking round the garden examining the house appraisingly, like an architect. Then he began a conversation.

"Your mother died there, in the upper room, behind closed shutters."

"No," I said, thinking back. "She died downstairs in the parlor that Nunu now occupies."

"Interesting," he said. "I had forgotten."

Then he threw away his cigarette, stood up, took a few firm strides to the wall, and tapped the bricks, shaking his head.

"A little damp," he said in a disapproving but abstract tone.

"We had it fixed last year," I said, still lost in my memories.

He came back to me and looked deep into my eyes. He remained silent for a long a time. We gazed at each other under half-closed eyelids, carefully and curiously. His expression was solemn now, devout.

"One question, Esther," he said quietly and solemnly. "Just one question."

I closed my eyes, feeling hot and dizzy. The dizziness lasted a few moments. I put out my hand as if to defend myself. It's starting, I thought. My god, he wants to ask me something. But what? Maybe he wants to know how the whole thing happened? Whether it was I who lacked courage? No, now I have to answer. I took a deep breath, ready to answer his question.

"Tell me, Esther," he asked quietly, soulfully. "Does this house still have a mortgage?"

II

*T*he events of the morning, at least all those that followed this last sentence, have grown a little confused in my mind. "Mister" Endre chose that moment
to come over. Lajos was confused and started lying, very
loudly. Like someone who wants to overcome his fear
by shouting, he began in high C with false geniality and
a hollow superior air that had no effect on Endre. He
grabbed Endre's arm in "dear old friend" manner and
regaled him with some amusing anecdotes, behaving
entirely as if he were a warmly awaited, high-ranking
guest in the house of his social inferiors. Endre calmly
heard him through. Endre is the one man in the world
Lajos fears, the one utterly impervious to his magic,
who has an inner indifference to the kind of rays and
spells that, he believes, emanate from Lajos and affect

everything, even animals and inanimate objects. Endre listened carefully to Lajos, fully aware of his professional secrets, knowing how he performed his conjuring tricks, quite prepared for Lajos to produce the national tricolor flag from his hat or make the fruit bowl disappear from the middle of the table. He listened with polite attention, without rancor, clearly interested in what Lajos had to say. It was as if he himself were saying: Show me another trick. As for Lajos, he took a brief rest between tricks, flicking the odd careful sidelong glance at Endre.

I think I was the only one to spot the panic. Tibor and Laci were absorbed by the sheer beauty of the performance. Later, in the afternoon, I learned that little Éva had also noticed Lajos's confusion. Endre seemed to know some simple undeniable truth with which he could pin Lajos down anytime he chose. But he was not mocking, nor was he in the least unfriendly.

"So, Lajos, you've come," he said, and they shook hands.

That was all. Lajos gave a nervous laugh. No doubt he would have worked with fewer constraints had there been no witnesses to his moment of departure. But ultimately, as we knew, it had been he who had invited Endre "in an official capacity." He had expressly requested, in writing, that Endre should not be absent that day, since he wanted to talk to him. Endre came with Lajos's letter of invitation in his pocket and stood in the garden, fat and placid, mildly blinking, patiently listening to Lajos without any sense of superiority, with the unshakable confidence of people who disdain the use of their full powers, knowing that one glance, one raised admonitory finger, and Lajos would immediately fall silent, slink away, and the show be over. Nevertheless, it seemed that Lajos could not do without this inconvenient witness. It was as if, after a long internal struggle, he had decided to face the truth—Lajos having always regarded Endre as the representative of truth, remorseless as judge and witness, a ruthless, antagonistic object to whom Lajos's spells were like water off a duck's back—and say: Let's get this over and done with. That is how Lajos regarded the aging figure of Endre.

It was only some three or four years since Endre had aged. Everything that was serious and heavy in his appearance and nature, the mysterious resistance to the world that never let anyone get close to him, the priestly air and the silent watchfulness that was characteristic of him from his earliest youth, sometimes made it hard, even for a stranger, to connect with him. He wasn't exactly unfriendly, it was just that one always felt he knew something about the world that defied all its laws and that he kept that secret to himself. His goodness was heavy, cautious, and clumsy.

Even now he was looking at Lajos like someone who

knows everything but feels no temptation either to judge or excuse him. The phrase "So, Lajos," with which, after twenty years, he greeted him, was not exactly condescending, not proud or severe, and yet I saw how the words discomposed Lajos, how he was glancing around nervously, in a funk, wiping his brow with a handkerchief. They talked together about politics and about the funeral. Then Endre, having seen and heard enough, gave a shrug, sat down on the bench, and crossed his hands over his belly, old-gentleman fashion. The day was well into the late afternoon, and once he had checked the deeds by which I empowered Lajos to sell the house, he had nothing more to say to anyone.

Naturally, we were all aware that Lajos wanted my life, or, more precisely, Nunu's life, that he wanted to rob me of my peace. The house was still there providing a roof above our heads, a little battered by time but, despite everything, still fortress-like: the house was the last object of value we possessed that Lajos had not yet taken away, and now he had come for it. The moment I received the telegram I knew he was after the house; one doesn't think such things in words, one just knows. I carried on deceiving myself to the last. Endre knew, so did Tibor. Later we were astonished at how cheaply and easily we surrendered to Lajos and accepted the fact that in life there are no halfway solutions, and the process having begun fifteen years ago simply had to be finished. Lajos knew it too. He had established that the house was a touch damp and having done so immediately talked about something else, as if the most important part of his business was concluded and there was no point wasting words on details. Tibor and Laci stood by inquisitively. Sometime later, before dinner, a tailor arrived, Lajos's old tailor, and bowing and scraping in embarrassment handed over a twenty-five-year-old bill. Lajos embraced him and sent him away. The gentlemen drank vermouth, talked in loud voices, and laughed a great deal at Lajos's anecdotes. We sat down to dinner in an excellent mood.

12

The only thing I couldn't understand was what the strange woman was doing here. She was too old and plainly dressed to be Lajos's lover. It took me a while to understand that the young man in the leather coat who had been the first to get out of the red car, who had mumbled a few courtesies of greeting and then said nothing the rest of the time, communicating only with his lion-headed dog, was the woman's son. There was something contrary to our agreement here. The young man was blond, light blond, a kind of silvery blond; it was as if his face were naked, his eyelashes almost invisible against the pale skin. He was constantly blinking. His hair was curly and woolly in texture like an old African's. Later he put on a pair of dark blue glasses and practically disappeared behind the dark lenses. It was only toward evening that I discovered that this young man was Éva's fiancé and that the woman, a rather respectable sort of woman who tended to mix badly pronounced French words in her conversation, had for years been Lajos's housekeeper. I understood nothing of this in the confusion of the first few hours.

The woman, whom the children addressed as Olga, was, if anything, rather melancholy and embarrassed. She made no effort to press her company on us and, after the introductions, sat quietly at the breakfast table fiddling with her parasol and gazing at her plate. I took her for an adventuress at first. But my later impression was that if she was an adventuress she was a tired and ill-tempered one, someone who no longer believed in the adventure and would happily give it all up to settle in some quiet occupation like crochet or embroidery. Occasionally she gave a bitter smile that bared her yellow, masculine teeth. When I came face-to-face with her I didn't know what to say. We took stock of each other, smiling at first then without smiles, with hard looks and undisguised suspicion. A cloud of sweetish perfume billowed from her dress and painted yellow hair.

"Dear Esther," she said.

I resisted the intimacy and loudly answered:

"Madam."

I laughed. The house was all but dissolving in those hours before lunch, becoming no more than a splendid mirage. Doors were slamming. Lajos took out a box from which he produced a tortoise and was demonstrating how it responded to music, moving when he whistled, sticking out its wrinkled neck and making a hissing noise by way of communication. He had brought the creature with him as a conversation piece, an accessory, as evidence of his triumph as a genius animal trainer. The tortoise was a great success. We all stood around enthusing about Lajos's performance, and even the solemn Endre succumbed to his curiosity.

Lajos went on to distribute presents: a wristwatch for Laci, two rare French editions of poetry, bound in leather, for Nunu (he had garnished the gift with a presentation verse of his own, indifferent to the fact that Nunu couldn't read French), Tibor and Endre received expensive foreign cigars, and I got a lilac silk shawl. The excitement was general, constantly at boiling point. There were strangers gawping over the fence, so we retreated into the house. The house was filling up with the aroma of hot seasoned food that always carries an immemorial sense of the simple delights of life along with something of its haste, conjuring the tinkle of cutlery, the slamming of doors, the clatter of plates, the distant chatter of arriving guests, faint childish screams, all amounting to some physical or musical *fanfare* to declare that life was a miracle to be celebrated! Which was exactly what I saw whatever way I turned. The unknown woman sat down in a corner and talked in a flat voice.

She told me how she had first met Lajos eight years before when she left her husband. Her son worked in an office; she did not say precisely where or what kind. I had never in my life seen people like the woman and her son at close quarters. I had leafed through magazines where there were photographs of what the young were up to, or a species of youth, the kind of people who danced in jackets with padded shoulders in the lobbies of hotels or flew airplanes or dashed off somewhere on a motorcycle with young women whose skirts fluttered above the knee on the pillion seat. I am of course aware that there is another species of the young who are perfectly real people. The former is just my caricature of unnerving aliens of whom I know next to nothing but who live on in my memory and imagination. All I know is that they are no longer anything to do with me. Beyond the confusion, beyond my ignorance, when I am in their presence I know that I have no means of communicating with them; they are the species of motoring and dancing humanity I see on movie screens, who are not included in the contract my parents and I had established with society.

There was something unusual about the boy; he might have been the hero of a novel, most likely a detective story. He said little, and when he spoke he stared at the ceiling and pronounced each syllable distinctly, almost singing the words. He was as melancholy as his mother; both exuded a dreary sadness. I had never before been with people who were so insultingly, so brazenly alien. He didn't smoke, he didn't drink. He wore a thin gold bracelet on his left wrist. Sometimes he raised his hand so suddenly it looked as though he wanted to hit someone; then, with a stiff mechanical movement, he would push the bracelet farther up his arm. I discovered he had not long passed thirty and was a secretary of some sort at the headquarters of one of the political parties, but when he took off his dark blue glasses and surveyed the people and objects in the room his watery eyes made him look even older than Lajos.

Why do you bother with them! I thought. But I couldn't help noticing that he kept an eye on the company. I didn't even like his name, the rather common Béla. It meant nothing to me. I always have a strong reaction to names, liking or hating them. It is an unjustified, crude feeling. But it is just such feelings that determine our relationship to the world, our loves and hates. I couldn't give him very much attention, since his mother completely occupied mine. Without any invitation whatsoever she gave me her life. The story was one long catalog of complaint, a shrill cry of accusation directed at authorities both earthly and heavenly, at men and women, at relatives and lovers, at children and husbands. The accusations were rendered in a flat, even voice, in smooth, round sentences, as if she were reciting a text she knew by heart. Everyone had deceived her, everyone was against her, and, in the end, they had all left her; that, at least, was what I gathered from her philippics. I occasionally shuddered: it was like being addressed by a lunatic. Then, without pausing, she got on to the subject of Lajos. She spoke cynically and confidentially. I couldn't bear her manner. It humiliated me to think that Lajos required accomplices of this kind to call on me, that this person had some kind of rank. I stood up with Lajos's gift, the lilac silk shawl, in my hand.

"We don't know each other," I said. "Perhaps we should not be speaking like this."

"Oh," she said calmly, quite indifferent to my concern. "We will have plenty of time to talk about it. We will get to know each other, dear Esther."

She lit a cigarette and blew a long line of smoke, gazing so assuredly through the cloud at me it seemed she must have already arranged everything. It was all decided: she knew something I didn't, and there was nothing I could do except give in.

13

There are three conversations I should note here. That was precisely how many took place that afternoon. Éva was first at my door, followed by Lajos, and lastly by the "officially invited" Endre. After lunch the guests dispersed. Lajos lay down to have a nap, as naturally as if he were at home and would not be diverted from his domestic habits. Gábor and the strangers set off in the car to see the church, the neighborhood, and the local ruins, returning only at dusk. Éva, however, came to my room straight after the meal. I stood with her by the window, cupped her face in my hands, and gazed at her a long time. She gazed back steadily with her clear blue eyes.

"You have to help us, Esther," she said eventually. "Only you can help us."

She had a sweet singsong voice, like a schoolgirl. She

only reached up to my shoulder. I hugged her but then felt the whole scene was a little too sentimental, and was glad when she gently disengaged herself, moved to the sideboard, lit a cigarette, gave a light cough, and, as if freed from an embarrassing, slightly disingenuous situation, examined the objects and framed photographs arranged on the flat surface. This shelf, the upper half of the sideboard, was a sacred place for me, the kind of thing the Chinese think of as a household shrine, before which they bow and honor their ancestors. Everyone I loved or was close to me stood there in a long row, each of them looking at me. I went over to her and watched her eyes moving along them.

"That's Mama," she said quietly but with evident delight. "How beautiful she is. She must have been younger there than I am now."

An eighteen-year-old Vilma gazed back at us, a little chubby, dressed in the garments of the time, in white lace with high black boots, her hair undone, curled, and combed over her brow, carrying flowers and a fan. The picture must have been for an occasion, since it was a touch self-conscious and unnatural. Only the dark, questioning eyes betrayed something of the later angry, passionate Vilma.

"Do you remember her?" I asked, and knew my voice was not quite steady.

"Vaguely," she replied. "Someone comes into my room in the dark and leans over me with a warm familiar scent. That's all I remember. I was three years old when she died."

"Three and a half," I say, flustered.

"Yes. But really I only remember you. You are always adjusting something on me, my dress or my hair, and you are always in my room, you always have something to do there. Then you too disappear. Why did you leave, Esther?"

"Hush," I say. "Hush, Éva. You don't yet understand."

"Yet? . . ." she asked, and started to laugh in the same singsong way, the laugh a little forced, too drawn out, too theatrical. Everything she said seemed extraordinarily important, too carefully composed. "Are you still playing at being the little mama, Esther, dear?" she said, kindly, superior, and compassionate. And now it was she who, with an adult movement, put her arm round my shoulder, led me over to the couch, and sat me down.

This time we looked at each other like two women, women who know or guess each other's secrets. Suddenly a hot flush of excitement ran through me. Vilma's daughter! I thought. The daughter of Vilma and Lajos. I felt I was blushing with a jealousy that sprang from somewhere so deep it shocked me with its energy and power: it was as if a jealous voice were shouting in me. I didn't want to listen to it. She could have been your daughter! was what the voice was crying. Your daughter, the meaning of your life. Why has she come back? Agitated, I bowed my head, burying my face in my hands. The significance of the moment balanced the shame I felt even as I was moving. I knew I was betraying my secret, that I was being watched by someone who was pitilessly observing my shame and discomfort; that the young woman who might have been my daughter had no sympathy and was not about to save me in this sorry situation. After an interval that seemed to be infinitely long I heard her mature, strange, self-aware, indifferent voice again.

"You shouldn't have gone away, Esther. I know it can't have been easy with Father. But you should have known you were the only one who might have helped him. And then there were Gábor and me. You simply left us to our fates. It was like abandoning two children at the gate of a house. Why did you do it?"

And when I remained silent, she calmly added:

"You did it out of revenge. Why look at me like that? You were wicked and acted out of revenge. You were the only woman who had any power over Father. You were the only woman he ever loved. No, Esther, that much I know, at least as well as you and Father. What happened between you? I have thought about it a long time. I had time to think, an entire childhood. Believe me, that childhood was not particularly happy. Do you know the details? I am quite prepared to tell you. I came here to tell you. And, at the end of my story, to ask you to help. I feel you owe us that much."

"Anything," I said, "I'll do anything to help you."

I straightened up. The difficult moment had passed.

"Look, Éva," I went on, and now I too felt calm. "Your father is a really interesting, very talented man. But all those things you were talking about just now have become a little confused in his memory. You should be aware that your father is quick to forget. Please don't think I am criticizing him. He can't help it. That's his nature . . ."

"I know," she answered. "Father never remembers reality. He is a poet."

"Yes," I said, my heart a little lighter. "He might be a poet. Reality gets confused in his mind. That's why you shouldn't believe everything he says . . . his memory is poor. The time you are talking about was the most difficult, most unbearably painful, most complicated part of my life. You say revenge! What kind of word is that to use? Who taught you to use it? You know nothing. Everything your father says about that time is fantasy, pure fantasy. But I do remember the reality. It was rather different. I owe nothing to anyone."

"But I have read the letters," she retorted in a matter-of-fact way.

Now I fell silent. We looked at each other.

"What letters?" I asked, astonished.

"The letters, Esther," she sharply retorted. "Father's letters, the ones he wrote to you at the time. You know, when he used to visit the house, when he was obsessed with you, saying that you should run away together because he couldn't go on otherwise, could no longer keep up appearances, that he couldn't cope with Vilma, who was stronger than he was and who hated you, Esther . . . because Mother did hate you. . . . Why? Because you were younger? Or more beautiful, or more real? Only you can answer that."

"What are you talking about, Éva," I cried, and shook her by the arm. "What letters? What is this nonsense?"

She freed her arm, stroked her forehead with her gentle childlike hands, and stared at me with big wide eyes.

"Why are you lying?" she asked, her voice cold and hard.

"I have never lied," I answered.

She shrugged.

"I have read the letters," she said, and folded her arms like a magistrate. "They were lying in the cupboard for ages, in the cupboard where Mama kept her underwear, where you hid them—you know, in that rosewood box . . . It is hardly three years since I found them."

I felt myself going pale, the blood draining from my face.

"Tell me what they say," I demanded. "Think what you like, think me a liar, but tell me everything you know about those letters."

"I don't understand," she said sharply, now that it was her turn to be surprised. "I am talking about the three letters that Father wrote you when he was engaged to Mama, begging you to release him from his emotional prison, because he loved only you. The last letter was dated just before the wedding. I compared the dates. It's the letter where he writes that he can't speak to you directly because he hasn't the strength and is ashamed on account of Mama. I don't think Father has ever written a more sincere letter. He writes that he is a crushed, injured man, that he trusts only you, that only you can give him back his self-respect and sanity. He begs you to elope with him, to abandon all else, to go abroad with him; that he puts his life into your hands. It is a letter of despair. It is impossible that you should not remember it, Esther. It is impossible, isn't it? For some reason you don't want to discuss these letters with me . . . . maybe they are painful on account of Mama, or you simply want to hide the whole thing from me. I understood everything once I read these letters. I saw my father in quite a different light from that time on. It's enough that once in one's life one should strive to be strong and good. It wasn't his fault that he failed. Why didn't you answer?"

"What should I have answered?" I asked, in the same flat, indifferent voice anyone might use in admitting that they had lied, and if I had genuinely known of these letters.

"What? . . . My god! You should have answered *something*. These were the sort of letters people get just once in a lifetime. He wrote that he would wait till the morning for your answer. If you did not answer he would know you lacked the strength . . . in which case he had no choice but to remain here and marry Mama. But he couldn't speak to you about this. He was afraid you would not believe him because he had often lied before. I cannot know what happened between you . . . I don't even have any right to ask. But you did not answer his letter, and soon everything went terribly wrong. Don't be cross, Esther . . . now that it is all over I think you were partly responsible for what happened."

"When did your father write those letters?"

"The week before the wedding."

"Where did he address them?"

"Where? Here, home, to your house. You lived here then together with Mama."

"You found them in a rosewood box?"

"Yes, in a box, in the cupboard where the underwear was kept."

"Did anyone have a key to that cupboard?"

"Only you. And Father."

What could I have answered? I let go of her arm, stood up, went over to the sideboard, and picked up Vilma's portrait and gazed at it a while. It had been a long time since I had held the picture in my hands. Now I stared at those familiar and yet terrifyingly strange eyes and suddenly I understood.

14

My sister Vilma hated me. Éva was right, there had been bad blood between us for as long as I can remember, a nameless dark fury the reasons for which had disappeared over the years. Nothing can explain this mutual hatred—for the fact is that I hated her as much as she did me—nor did either of us ever seek to explain it. I cannot be more precise in specifying whether this or that act of hers did the damage; she would have said something different anyway, and that was why we were so much against each other. She was always the stronger, even in matters of hatred. If someone were to have asked her why she hated me so relentlessly, she could have spat out a long list of accusations complete with reasons, but none of them would have explained the hatred. We put aside the excuses. There remained the fury, the hot thick feeling that floods every inch of the human landscape with its muddy slime, and when Vilma died there were no family ties left, only a blank floodplain of hatred.

I held the picture close to my nearsighted eyes and examined it carefully. How strong the dead are! I thought helplessly. At that particular moment Vilma was alive in a mysterious form of being that the dead assume when they want to intervene in our lives, the dead whom we believe are buried under mounds of earth and bound by the chains of decay. But come the day, and they appear and act. Maybe this is that day, Vilma's day, I thought. And I remembered the afternoon when she was dying, when she could only recognize what was around her for a few seconds at a time, when I was weeping at her bedside, waiting for her to speak, to bid farewell or pronounce a word of reconciliation, all the while knowing that I hadn't forgiven her, not even then, on death's threshold, any more than had she in her swoon of death forgiven me. I covered my face with my hands and wept. And then she spoke. *You'll think of me yet,* said she, no longer in her right mind. She has forgiven me! I thought, hoping it might be so. But what I secretly felt was, *She is threatening me.* And then she died. After the funeral I stayed in the apartment for months. One couldn't leave the children alone to fend for themselves. Lajos traveled abroad and was away for a few months. I stayed in the empty apartment waiting for something.

But as for Vilma's cupboard, that particular cupboard where Éva was later to find the letters, I never once opened it. If someone were to ask why, I might give the righteous answer, proclaiming in ringing words that I had no right to meddle in the affairs of the dead. The truth is I was a coward. I was afraid of what might be in the cupboard, afraid of the memory of Vilma. And that was because, having died and therefore unilaterally brought an end to our eternal passionate dialogue and concluded the quarrel between us, she seemed to have placed any memory we might have shared, any ambition or temper we might have had in common, under a peculiar ban. Lajos went away after the funeral and I lived there with the children in an apartment where nothing belonged to me and yet everything had been partly stolen from me, where all useful items seemed to have been stamped by some mysterious executor—at that stage it was only the presence of executors of that kind we detected in the apartment, the real, the everyday, the official executors appearing only later, bearing bills for Lajos's debts—that was where I ran the household without daring to touch anything, feeling it was not mine, and where I brought up the children more timidly than any professional governess. Everything in the apartment was against me, everything under ban, everything exuded the strange, hostile quality that determines one's deeper sense of what is mine and what is yours in life. Nothing that remained here was mine. Vilma took it all with her, everything I would have wanted; she ruined everything, forbade everything I desired. She ruled over us with the despotic power only the dead can exercise. I put up with it for a while. I was waiting for Lajos, waiting for a miracle.

He rarely wrote while traveling abroad; at most he sent postcards. By that time he was putting on an act again; this time was "one of the turning points" of his life, a decisive moment he had to seize with both hands in a grand gesture: he had to be dressed to perfection for the part. The proper dress was mourning wear, the decisive moment the journey abroad. He set out like one who could not bear the pain, who had to escape his memories.

I think the truth was that he had a marvelous time amusing himself in those foreign cities, establishing business contacts—"burying himself in work," as he put it—in other words, going to the occasional museum or library and spending the rest of the time sitting around in cafés and restaurants, his contacts mainly sentimental. The soul of Lajos is made of flexible stuff, I thought. But in the months I waited for him I realized that I could not live with him, that something was missing in him, in his spirit, in his very being, some bonding agent without which you cannot form human relationships. His tears were real tears, but they did not dissolve anything in him, no memory, no pain: Lajos was always fully committed to delight or melancholy but actually felt nothing at all. There was something inhuman in all this. When he returned a few months later I did not wait for him but went home a few days before, leaving the children in the care of a dependable woman, writing Lajos a letter in which I said I did not want the role of pretend-mother, I wanted to know nothing about him and never wished to see him again. I received no answer to this letter. In the first few weeks—well, the first few years—I was waiting for him to answer, but later I understood that he could not answer, that the world in which we had lived together had crumbled away. After that I expected nothing from him.

Now when Éva was speaking of these unknown letters in such passionate and accusing tones, I suddenly remembered the rosewood box. The box was in fact mine, a present from Lajos for my sixteenth birthday, but Vilma had asked me for it. I was not happy giving it up. I didn't know Lajos properly then, and was not truly aware of my feelings for him. Vilma begged me for the box, and in the end I surrendered it, reluctantly but without putting up much resistance; I must have gotten bored with her pleading. Vilma was always asking me for my things, anything I had been given: clothes, books, musical scores, anything at all she thought might be treasured or of value to me. That's how she got the rosewood box. I protested for a while, then grew tired and gave in; I had to give it to her because she was simply stronger. Later, once I suspected that there might be something between Lajos and me, I begged in desperation to have the box back, but Vilma lied that she had lost it. This box, inlaid with rosewood, made of plywood and veneer, scented with spices with a slightly choking smell, lined in red silk, was the only gift I ever received from Lajos. I never considered the ring a real present. The box vanished from my life. Then there it was again, decades later, in Éva's story, with these strange contents, the three letters from Lajos before his marriage, begging me to elope with him, to save him. I put the picture back where it was.

"What do you people want from me?" I asked, and leaned against the sideboard.

15

"Look, Esther," she said, a little confused now, and lit another cigarette. "Father will tell you everything. I think he's right. You may think a great deal has happened since you left us, and indeed a great deal has happened, not always for the best. I don't remember the earliest days. Then we went to school and life became exciting. We moved apartments yearly, not just apartments but schools and nannies too. Those nannies . . . my god . . . as you can imagine Father was none too choosy. Most of them ran off, taking a few of our possessions with them, or it was we who ran off, leaving home and furniture behind; we went from one rented apartment to another. One time, when I would have been about twelve years old, we were living in hotel rooms. It was such an interesting life. The headwaiter dressed us, we shared lessons with the elevator boy, and when Father disappeared for a few days the chambermaids would look after us and see to our education. There were times when we ate sea crab day after day and other times when we hardly ate anything. Father is very fond of crab. That was our upbringing. Other children are brought up on sour milk or vitamins . . . But we generally had a good time. Only later, when Father's fortunes were on the rise and we reverted to respectable middle-class life, renting an apartment, managing a household, when Father set out on some new venture— and even as a child I trembled at Father's ventures—we occasionally wept to remember our hotel days, because even in our "respectable life" we were living like nomads in a desert. Father is not really an urban creature, you know. No, don't protest, I think I might know him better than you do. There is nothing of the materialist in Father, possessions mean nothing to him, he doesn't even mind whether he has a roof over his head or not. There is something in him of the hunter-gatherer, who rises in the morning, gets on his horse—he always kept a car even at the worst of times, usually driving it himself—and sets out into his own patch of savannah or forest, which in Father's case was the city, sniffs the air, stays on the alert, hunts down a suitably large banknote, roasts it, and offers everyone a bite; but then, while there is anything left of the prize, for days or even weeks on end, he is not interested in anything else . . . And, when it comes down to it, this is what we love in Father, and what you too love, Esther. Father is capable of discarding a piano or a decent job the way other people throw away used gloves; he has no respect for objects and market value, you know. This is something we, as women, cannot understand . . . I have learned a great deal from Father, but his real secret—his carelessness, his inner detachment—I cannot learn. He does not feel closely bound to anything, the only thing he's interested in is danger, life being the most peculiar danger . . . God alone knows, God alone can understand this . . . He needs this danger, this life among people but without human ties; he breaks ties out of curiosity and absent-mindedly throws them away. Did you not realize this when . . . ? I mean, did you not feel it? Even as a child I felt we were meant to live in a tent, a migrant tribe traveling through country that was sometimes dangerous, sometimes pleasant, Father with bow and quiver in his hand going ahead, spying out the terrain, dashing to telephones, listening, watching certain signs, then suddenly full of energy, fully alert, and tensed for action . . . elephants approaching the drinking pool, Father in his covert raising the bow. Are you laughing at me?"

"No," I replied, my throat dry. "Carry on. I won't laugh."

"Men, you know," she said in a wise pedagogic manner with a light sigh.

I did laugh. But I immediately grew serious again. I couldn't help but notice that Éva, Vilma's daughter, this child with whom I had lightheartedly adopted an adult, grown-up-woman tone, knew something about men, certainly something more and more certainly than I did, I who could have been her mother. I scolded myself for laughing.

"Yes, yes," she said innocently, and opened her big blue eyes to indicate her seriousness. "Men. There are such men, men unbound by family, possessions, or territory. They would have been hunters or fishermen in the past. Sometimes Father was away for months and then we were educated in institutions run by nuns who were good-natured if a little scared but who tried to keep us in order in much the same way as if they had found us abandoned by the roadside, as if bits of the jungle were still sticking to our hair, as if we had spent our time dining with monkeys off trees bearing loaves of bread. You see, that is the kind of colorful childhood we enjoyed . . . Not that I'm complaining. Please don't think I am complaining about Father. I love him, and I think he was nicest to me when he returned from one of his longer excursions a little exhausted, utterly broke, looking as if he had been fighting wild animals. It was really good at such times, for a while at least. On Sunday mornings he would take us to the museum and then to the sweetshop and the cinema. He would ask to look at our exercise books, clip on his monocle, and would chide and teach us with a solemn frown . . . It was all most amusing, Father as schoolmaster, can you imagine?"

"Yes," I said. "The poor thing."

But I didn't know who I felt more sorry for, the children or Lajos, nor did Éva ask. Now she was clearly absorbed in her memories. She continued in a friendly, easy manner.

"Actually, we didn't have too bad a time of it. That is, until one day the woman arrived."

"What woman?" I asked, striving to maintain a quiet conversational tone.

She shrugged.

"Fate," she pouted. "You know. Fate, the lady arriving at just the right time, at the very last moment . . ."

"What moment?" I asked, my mouth dry.

"The moment Father began to age. The moment the hunter notices his eye is not as sharp as it was, that his hand is trembling. One day Father took fright."

"What frightened him?"

"Old age. Himself. There's nothing sadder than when a man of his sort grows old, Esther. Then anyone, anyone at all can take advantage of him."

"What has she done to him?"

We spoke quietly, whispering like accomplices.

"She controls him," she said. Then, after a few moments: "We owe her money. Have you heard? I am engaged to him."

"Her son?"

"Yes."

"Do you love him?"

"No."

"Then why are you marrying him?"

"We have to save Father."

"What do you know about him?"

"Something bad. He has bills in his hand."

"Do you love someone else?"

Now it was her turn to fall silent. She stared at her pink-lacquered fingernails. Then, wise and mature, she quietly added: "I love Father. There are two people in the world who love him: you, Esther, and I. Gábor doesn't count. He is quite different."

"You don't want to marry the son?"

"Gábor is much calmer," she said, avoiding the answer. "It's as if he had locked himself away through a kind of deafness. He doesn't want to hear anything and seems not to see what is happening around him. It's his way of defending himself."

"There is someone else," I ventured and stepped closer to her. "Someone you love, and if it were possible to arrange things . . . somehow . . . it wouldn't be easy . . . and you should know, Éva, that I have little now, that we, Nunu and Laci and I, are poor now . . . but I might know someone who might help you."

"Oh, you could help, all right," she said in her cold voice again, with careless certainty as if dropping an aside. But it was some time since she had looked into my eyes. She was standing with her back to the window, and I couldn't see her face. The sky had grown gray since lunch, and through the window I could see dense dark September clouds gathering above the garden. The room floated in a half-light. I went over to the window and closed one of the open casements, afraid that someone might overhear us in the heavy silence before the rain.

"You must tell me," I said, my heart racing in a way it had not done for a very long time, the last time perhaps on the night when Mother died. "If you want to escape—you and your father—from these people, you must tell me if there is someone you love . . . If money can help . . . Now tell me."

"I think, Esther," she said, her eyes cast down on the

floor in her innocent schoolgirl voice, "that money, that is to say money alone, can no longer help. We need you too. Though Father knows nothing about this," she hastily added, almost frightened.

"About what?"

"This . . . what I told you."

"What is it you want?" I asked impatiently, raising my voice.

"I want to save Father," she dully replied.

"From these people?"

"Yes."

"And you want to save yourself?"

"If possible."

"You don't love him?"

"No."

"You want to get away?"

"Yes."

"Where?"

"Abroad. Far away."

"Is someone waiting for you?"

"Yes."

"Yes," I repeated, my heart lighter, and sat down exhausted. I pressed my hands to my heart. I felt dizzy again, as I always do when I step out of the shadow world of pointless watching and waiting and come face-to-face with reality. How much simpler reality is! Éva loves somebody and wants to join him: she wants to live a decent, honest life. And I have to help her. Yes, with everything at my disposal. Almost greedily, I asked her:

"What can I do, Éva?"

"Father will tell you," she replied with difficulty, as if reluctant to pronounce the words. "He has a plan . . . I think, they have plans. You'll get to hear them, Esther. That's their affair and yours. But you could help me particularly, if you wanted to. There is something in this house that is mine. As far as I know, it is mine . . . Excuse me, you see I am blushing. It's very difficult to talk about it."

"I don't understand," I said, and felt my hands grow cold. "What do you mean?"

"I need money, Esther," she said now, her voice breaking and raw, as if she were attacking me. "I need money to get away."

"Yes, of course," I said, puzzled. "Money . . . I am sure I can get hold of some money. I am pretty sure Nunu can too . . . Maybe I can talk to Tibor. But Éva," I said, as if coming to my senses, disillusioned and help-less, "I am afraid that what I can put together will not amount to very much."

"I don't need your money," she said, cold and proud. "I want nothing that is not mine. I want only that which Mother left me."

Suddenly her eyes were burning and accusing as she looked directly at me.

"Father said you were looking after my inheritance. That is all I have left of Mother. Give me back the ring, Esther. Now, immediately. The ring, you hear?"

"Yes, the ring," I said.

Éva was looking at me so aggressively that I backed away. It so happened that I found myself standing by the sideboard in which I had hidden the fake ring. I had only to lean back, open the drawer, and hand the ring over, the ring that Vilma's daughter had demanded from me with such hatred in her voice. I stood there helpless, my arms folded, determined to keep the secret of Lajos's treachery.

"When did your father speak of the ring?" I asked.

"Last week," she said, and shrugged. "When he told me we were coming here."

"Did he talk about the value of the ring?"

"Yes. He had it looked at once. A long time ago, after Mother's death . . . before he gave it to you, he had it valued."

"And what is it worth?" I asked calmly.

"A lot," she said, her voice with that peculiar hoarseness again. "Thousands. Maybe even ten thousand."

"Yes," I said.

Then I said, and I wondered at how I could maintain such control and even sound somewhat superior: "You are not getting the ring, my girl."

"Is there no ring?" she asked, looking me over. Then, more quietly: "Is it that you don't have it, or that you won't give it to me?"

"I will not answer that question," I said, and stared straight in front of me. At that moment I felt Lajos silently enter, stepping as lightly as ever, so lightly he might have been onstage, and I knew he was somewhere near.

"Leave us alone, Éva," I heard him say. "I have some business with Esther."

I did not glance back. It was a long time before Éva—giving me a long dark look that was to show she did not trust me—slowly left the room, hesitating on the threshold, giving a shrug, then pacing rapidly away. But she drew the door closed quietly, as if not entirely certain. We stood in the room for a while without seeing each other. Then I turned and, for the first time in fifteen years, stood face-to-face, alone with Lajos.

16

*H*e looked at me and smiled a peculiar, modest smile as if to say: *You see, it's not such a big thing really!* It wouldn't have surprised me if he had rubbed his hands together at that point, like a satisfied businessman left to meet his family after a particularly good deal, contemplating ever new deals and ever more tempting offers in the exhilaration of the moment. There was not a trace of shame or doubt on his face. He was in a good mood, happy as a child.

"I slept really well, Esther," he said expansively. "It's as if I had come home at last."

When I did not answer he took my arm, led me to an easy chair, and courteously sat me down.

"Now at last I can look at you," he murmured. "You haven't changed. Time has stopped in this house."

It did not disturb him at all that I remained quiet.

He walked up and down, gazed at various photographs, occasionally smoothing his thinning gray mane of hair with a cheap, stagy gesture. He meandered around the room with no more care than if he had popped out twenty-five years ago because he needed to be somewhere but was back now, absentmindedly resuming a conversation out of mere good manners. He picked up an old Venetian drinking glass from the table and gazed at it in wonder.

"This is a present from your father. For your birthday, wasn't it? I remember," he said amicably.

"When did you sell the ring?" I asked.

"The ring?"

He looked at the ceiling with a studious, puzzled expression. His lips moved silently as if he were counting.

"I can't remember," he said, perfectly charming.

"A likely story, Lajos," I pressed him. "Think back. I am sure it will come to you."

"The ring, the ring," he obligingly repeated, shaking his head as if he would be delighted to satisfy someone's whim, a peculiarly whimsical curiosity of little significance.

"Really now, when did I sell that ring? I do believe it was a few weeks before Vilma died. You know, we were so short of money at the time . . . Doctors, social life . . . Yes, it must have been that year."

And he pinned his shining eyes on me, bright with innocence.

"But Esther," he went on, "why are you interested in the ring?"

"And then you gave me the copy. Remember?" I asked, and took a step toward him.

"I gave it to you?" he repeated mechanically, and instinctively took a step back. "I might have. Did I really give it to you?"

He was still smiling, but a little less certainly now. I went over to the sideboard, opened it, and went straight to the ring.

"You still don't remember?" I asked, and passed it over to him.

"Yes," he said quietly. "Now I remember."

"You sold the ring," I said. I too had instinctively dropped my voice, the way one does only when speaking of something deeply shameful that has to be kept secret, even from God perhaps. "And when we returned from the funeral you gave it to me with a grand gesture as Vilma's bequest, as the one family heirloom of any great value, as something I alone should have. I was a little surprised. I even protested, do you remember? But then I accepted it and promised you I would look after it and pass it on to Éva when she grew up and when she needed it. You still don't remember?"

"You promised that, did you?" he asked lightly.

"Well, give it to her if she asks for it now," he added over his shoulder. He had started to walk about again and had lit a cigarette.

"Last week you told Éva that I was looking after this ring for her. Éva needs money: she wants to sell the ring. The moment she goes to have it valued, she will find out it is a fake. Naturally, I am the only one who could have had it faked. That is your doing," I said hoarsely.

"Why?" he asked astonished. It was a simple question. "Why you? It could have been somebody else. Vilma, for example."

We stood silent.

"How low will you sink, Lajos?" I asked.

He blinked and examined the ash on his cigarette.

"What sort of question is that? How low will you sink?" he asked uncertainly.

"How low will you sink?" I repeated. "I imagine everyone has a kind of gauge, a spirit level that determines what is good and bad within them. It's universal, everything has a limit, everything that is to do with human relationships. But you have no gauge."

"Mere words," he said, and waved them away as if bored. "Gauges, levels. Good and bad. Mere words, Esther."

"Have you thought," he continued, "that the great majority of our actions are undertaken without reason and have no purpose? People do things that bring them neither gain nor joy. If you looked back on your life you would notice that you have done a good many things simply because they seemed impossible to do."

"That's a little too fancy for me," I said, depressed.

"Fancy? Nonsense! Just uncomfortable, Esther. There comes a time in life when a man grows tired of everything having a point. I have always loved doing those things that have no point, things for which there is no explanation."

"But the ring," I insisted.

"The ring, the ring!" he muttered, annoyed. "Let's not get started with the ring! Did I tell Éva that you were looking after the ring? I might have. Why would I have said it? Because it seemed the thing to say at the time, it was the simplest, the most reasonable thing. You bring up the ring, Laci talks about some bills . . . what do you want? That's all in the past, these things no longer exist. Life destroys everything. It's impossible to live all your life with a burden of guilt. What soul is as innocent as you describe? Who is so high and mighty that she has the right to stalk someone else all their life? Even the law understands the concept of obsolescence. It's only you people who insist on denying it."

"Don't you think you are being a little unfair?" I asked more quietly.

"Maybe," he said, also in a quieter voice. "Levels! Gauges of the soul! Please understand that there are no gauges in life. I might have said something to Éva, I might have made a mistake yesterday or ten years ago, something to do with money or rings or words. I have never in my life resolved on a course of action. Ultimately people are only responsible for the things they consciously decide to do . . . Actions? What are they? Instincts that take you by surprise. People stand there and watch themselves acting. It is intention, Esther, intention is guilt. My intentions have always been honorable," he declared with satisfaction.

"Yes," I replied, uncertain. "Your intentions might have been honorable."

"I know," he said, more gently now, a little wounded, "I know I am a misfit in the world. Should I change now, in my fifty-sixth year? I have never wanted anything but good for everyone. But the chances of good in this world are limited. One has to make life more beautiful, or else it's unbearable. That's why I said what I said to Éva about the ring. The possibility consoled her at the time. That's why I told Laci fifteen years before that I would repay him, though I knew I would never do so. That's why I promise people all kinds of things on the spur of the moment and know, as soon as I tell them, that I will never do what I promised. That's why I told Vilma I loved her."

"Why did you tell her?" I asked, surprised at how calm and detached I sounded.

"Because that was what she wanted to hear," he said without a thought. "Because she had staked her life on me telling her that. And because you did not stop me from saying it."

"I?" I whispered, confused, especially confused now because I was practically choking. "What could I have done?"

"Everything, Esther," he said, innocent as a newborn child. It was the old voice, the voice of his youth. "Everything. Why did you not answer my letters? Why did you not answer my letters while you still could have? Why did you forget the letters and leave them with us when you left? Éva found them."

He came over to me now, quite close, and leaned over me.

"Have you seen these letters?" I asked.

"Have I seen them? . . . I don't understand, Esther. I wrote them."

And I could tell by his voice that for once, perhaps for the first time in his life, he was not lying.

17

"*N*ow let me tell you something," he said, and, leaning against the sideboard with the photographs on it, he lit a cigarette and threw the match distractedly into the box holding people's calling cards. "Something happened between us that we can no longer settle by not speaking about it. One can remain silent all one's life about the most important things. People die in silence. But there may be occasions to speak, when one should not remain silent. I believe it was this kind of silence that might have been the original sin of which the Bible speaks. There is an ancient lie at the heart of life, and it can take a long time before a man notices it. Don't you want to sit down? Sit down, Esther, and hear me through. No, excuse me, this time, just this once, I would like to be judge and prosecutor. All this time you have been the judge. Sit down, please."

He spoke courteously but in an almost commanding manner.

"There you are," he said, and pushed a chair toward me. "Look, Esther, for twenty years we have been talking at cross-purposes. Things are not so simple. You have read out your list of charges against me—you and others—and they are indeed faults, alas, and perfectly true. You talk of rings and lies, of promises not kept, of bills that I have not paid. There is more, Esther, and worse. There's no point in telling it all . . . I make no excuses for myself . . . but details like this will no longer decide my future. I have always been a weak man. I would like to have achieved something in the world, and I believe I was not altogether without talent. But talent and ambition are not enough. I know now they are not enough. To be properly creative one needs something else . . . some special strength or discipline or a mixture of the two; the stuff, I think, they call character . . . And that quality, that talent, is something that is missing in me. It's like a strange deafness. It is as if I knew the music, the tune being played, precisely, but could not hear the notes. When I met you I was not quite so certain of what I am telling you now . . . I didn't even know that you represented character for me. You understand?"

"No," I honestly replied.

Somehow it was not his words that astonished me

but his voice, the way he spoke. I had not heard him speak like this before. He spoke like a man who . . . but it is almost impossible to pin the voice down. He spoke like a man who has seen or discovered something, some truth, or is on his way to doing so though he could not yet declare it, because he was getting ever closer and was shouting his impressions at the world for all he was worth. He spoke like a man who felt something. It was not a voice I was used to with him. I listened without speaking.

"It's so simple," he said. "You'll understand it straightaway. It was you: you were what I was missing, you were my character, my being. One recognizes this sort of thing. A man without character, or with an imperfect character, is morally something of a cripple. There are people like that, people who in every other respect are perfectly normal but for a missing arm or leg. Such people are given prostheses, an artificial arm or leg, and suddenly they are capable of working again, of being useful. Please don't be angry at my analogy, but you must have been a kind of artificial limb to me . . . a moral prosthesis. I hope I haven't offended you?" he asked tenderly, and leaned over to me.

"No," I said. "It is simply that I don't believe it, Lajos. There is no such thing as a prosthetic being. You can't graft the moral character of one person onto another. Forgive me, but these are just ideas."

"No, they are not just ideas. A moral character is not something you inherit but a quality you acquire. People are not born with morals. The morals of wild animals, the morals of children, are not the same as the morals of a sixty-year-old circuit judge in Vienna or Amsterdam. People acquire their moral characters in the same way as they acquire their mannerisms and their culture."—He was intoning like a priest.—"There are people who are more adept at moral character, yes indeed, there are moral geniuses just as there are musical and literary geniuses. You are such a moral genius, Esther; no, please don't deny it. I feel it in you. I am tone-deaf when it comes to issues of morality, practically illiterate. That is why I needed to be with you, or that at any rate is the chief reason, I think."

I was obstinate. "I don't believe it," I said, "but even if it were so, Lajos, you cannot want someone to act as moral nanny to all kinds of morally imperfect beings. A woman can't play moral nurse her whole life."

"A woman! A woman!" he said quickly, courteously waving my answer away. "I am talking about you, Esther. I mean you."

"A woman," I said, and felt the blood rush to my face. "I know you mean me. I have had enough of being the model for a false view of the world all my life. Get that into your head at last. There is no point in me saying it again . . . though maybe you are right, we cannot remain silent about this forever. I don't believe in your ideas, Lajos, I believe in reality. The reality is that you deceived me; once upon a time people might have put this in a more flowery, romantic way, such as: 'I was your plaything, your toy.' You are a strange gambler; you play with passions and people instead of cards. I was one of the queens in your hand. Then you stood up and went off elsewhere. Why? Because you grew bored. You had had enough and simply walked away. That's the truth. That is the terrible immoral truth. One can't throw a woman away the way one does a matchbox simply because one has passions, because that happens to be one's nature, because one finds it impossible being tied to a woman or because one is ambitious, or because everything and everyone is merely useful. I can even understand that . . . it is a low act with something human in it. But to discard someone out of sheer carelessness, that is lower than low. There is no excusing that, because it is inhuman. Do you understand now?"

"But I called you, Esther," he said quite quietly. "Don't you remember? Yes, I was weak. But then, at the last moment, I came to my senses and knew that only you could help me. I called you, I begged you. Don't you remember my letters?"

"I know nothing about any letters," I said, and was frightened to note how sharp my voice sounded, sharper than it had ever been, almost shrieking. "It's all lies. The letters are a lie, like the ring, like everything you ever said or promised me. I know nothing about the letters, I don't believe in them. Éva has only just told me that she had found letters like that . . . in the rosewood box . . . how should I know what is true in all this? I don't believe you. I don't believe Éva either. I don't believe in the past. It is all lies and conspiracies, a piece of theater full of stage properties, old letters and vows that were never made. I don't go to the theater nowadays, Lajos. I haven't been to a theater in fifteen years. I don't go out. I know the truth, do you understand? The truth. Look at me! This is the truth! Look into my eyes! I am old. We are at the end of life, as you yourself so grandly declared. Yes, it is the end, and you are the reason that this is the way it has passed, so empty, so false; it is why I stayed here, living alone like an old maid who is thrifty with her feelings but eventually buys a cat and a dog as pets . . . my pets are people."

"Yes," he admitted, bowing his head in guilt. "That is a very dangerous thing to do."

"Yes, dangerous," I repeated, instinctively more quietly now, then fell silent. I had never spoken for as long and as passionately as that at one go. I was quite out of breath.

"So, let us leave it," I said. Suddenly I felt weak. I did

not want to cry, so I sat there with my arms folded and my back straight, but I must have gone very pale because Lajos looked at me, concerned.

"Do you want a glass of water? Shall I call someone?"

"Don't call anyone," I said. "It's not important. It looks as though I am no longer as healthy as I was. Look, Lajos, while two people are still at the stage where one doubts the words of the other, then there is soil enough, however shallow, to build a relationship on. The soil may be marshland or loose sand. You know that what you build will eventually fall down, yet there is something in the enterprise that is real, human and destined. But those cursed by fate to build on you have a far worse time of it, because one day they are obliged to notice that they have built on mere air, on nothing. Some people lie because it's their nature, because they seek some advantage or spontaneously for a moment's excitement. But you lie the way rain rains: you can lie with tears, you can lie with your actions. It must be very difficult. There are times I think you're an absolute genius . . . the genius of lies. You look into my eyes or touch me, your tears welling, and I start to feel how your hand trembles, but all the time I know you are lying, that you have always lied, right from the first moment. Your life has been one long lie. I don't even believe in your death: that will be a lie too. Oh yes, you're a genius all right."

"Well, there you are," he replied calmly. "In any case, I have brought you the letters. I did, after all, write them for you. Here they are."

And with a simple courteous gesture he produced the three letters from his coat pocket and handed them over to me.

18

At that point I was not too concerned with the contents of the letters. I was fully aware of Lajos's capabilities as a letter writer. But I did have a thorough look at the envelopes. All three bore my name and address, the hand was clearly Lajos's, and the franking proved them to have been mailed to my address twenty-two years ago, the week before Vilma and Lajos were married. I am sure that I never received them. Somebody must have intercepted them. It wouldn't have been too difficult to steal them: it was always Vilma, endlessly curious about mail, who took the letters from the mailman, and it was she who had the key to the sideboard. I carefully examined the backs of the envelopes, then threw them down beside the other objects displayed on the sideboard, next to the photograph of Vilma.

"Don't you want to read them?" asked Lajos.

"No," I said. "Why? I believe they say what you told me they said. They are not of great importance. You," I said, almost crazy, pronouncing the words as if making a great discovery. "You can even make facts lie."

"You never received these letters?" Lajos asked calmly, as though he were not too concerned with my criticisms of him.

"Never."

"Who stole my letters?"

"Who stole them? Vilma. Who else? Who else would benefit from doing so?"

"Of course," he said. "It couldn't have been anyone but her."

He went over to the sideboard and took a good look at the stamps on the letter and the franking, then leaned closer to look at Vilma's picture, with a smile of good-natured interest, the cigar in his hand emitting clouds of curling smoke. He gazed at the picture fully absorbed, as though I was not in the room, wagging his head, then giving a low whistle of appreciation, the way one burglar might admire the work of another. He stood there, legs widely spaced, one hand in his coat pocket, the other with the smoking cigar, a satisfied professional.

"She made a good job of it," he said eventually, and

turned to me, stopping one step from me. "But in that case," he went on, "what is it you want from me? What is my crime? My debt? The great thing I failed to do? What is the lie? It's just details. But there was a moment," he pointed to the letters, "when I did not lie, when I put out my hands because I was dizzy, the way a high-wire walker starts to get dizzy. And you did not help me. No one lifted a finger. So I danced on as best I could, since a thirty-five-year-old man does not fancy falling from such a height . . . You know I'm not particularly given to sentimentality, that's right, I'm not even a passionate man. It was life that interested me . . . risks . . . the game, as you called it. I am not, nor have I ever been, the kind of man who stakes everything on a woman, on passion and sentiment . . . Nor was it any unstoppable tide of sentiment that swept me to you, I can tell you that now. You see, I don't want to make you cry, it's not that I want your heart to melt. That would be ridiculous. I did not come to beg. I came to demand. Do you understand now?" he asked quietly, amicable but solemn.

"Demand?" I said almost inaudibly. "That's interesting. Go on. Demand."

"Very well," he said. "I'll try. It is nothing I could put down on paper or go to the law with, of course. But there are other kinds of law. You may not realize it, but this is the moment you should become aware that beside the moral law there is another, just as binding, just as valid . . . how to put it? Are you beginning to suspect what it might be? There's a kind of self-knowledge people are usually very reluctant to bear. You should know that it is not only words, vows, and promises that bind people together, nor is it feelings or sympathies that determine the true nature of their relationship. There's something else, a law that is firmer and more severe, that determines whether one person is bound to another or not . . . It's like the law between fellow conspirators. That is the law that bound me to you. I knew about this law. Even twenty years ago, I knew. I knew as soon as I met you. There's no point in being modest now: I believe that of the two of us, Esther, it is I who am made of sterner stuff. That 'stuff' is not sterner in the sense that handbooks of moral guidance pretend. Nevertheless it is I, the faithless, the fly-by-night, the fugitive, who am more capable of remaining true to that law in both soul and will, this law of which you will find no trace in books or in the tables of the law but which is, nevertheless, the true law. And it is a very hard law . . . Listen. The law of life is that what is once begun has to be finished. This does not make for a particularly happy state of affairs. Nothing happens when it's supposed to: at the very moment when you have spent your precious time preparing to receive an important gift, life gives you nothing. This belatedness, this disorder, can hurt you for years. We think someone is just playing with us. But one day we notice that everything has been exactly as it is supposed to be, in perfect order, in perfect time . . . it is impossible for people to meet one day sooner than they are supposed to. They meet when they're ready for meeting . . . They're ready not necessarily by virtue of their whims and wishes but by virtue of something deeper, some undeniable stellar law, the way planets meet in infinite time and space, precise to within a microsecond, colliding at a unique moment, one in a billion years in the vastness of space. I don't believe in chance meetings. I am a man who knows a good number of women . . . forgive me, but this is an unavoidable part of what I have to say . . . I have met beautiful ones, high-spirited ones, in fact I have known some who were animated by some fire-breathing demon; I have known heroic women who could wade through Siberian snows in the company of a man, remarkable women who could help me and were prepared to share with me the terrible loneliness of existence for a while. Yes, I have known all these," he said quietly, reminiscing, more to himself than to me.

"I am so glad," I said stiffly when he stopped, "so delighted that you have chosen to come back to me and regale me with your acquaintances."

But I immediately regretted the words. They were unbecoming to me, and unbecoming to what Lajos had just said too. He looked at me calmly and nodded, bemused.

"What was I to do when it was always you I was waiting for?" he asked almost tenderly. It was simple. It was elegantly and modestly said.

"What was I to do?" he said more loudly. "And what can you do with this belated confession that, at our time of life, has neither meaning nor virtue. One shouldn't say things like this. But the manners of *should* or *should not* are worthless when discussing the truth. See, Esther, a leave-taking can be just as mysterious and exciting as a first meeting . . . I have long known this. Revisiting someone we loved is not the same as 'returning to the scene of the crime,' 'driven by an irresistible compulsion,' as the detective stories have it. All my life I have loved only you, not out of some strict necessity, nor quite according to the laws of logic . . . Then something happened, not only the accident of the letters, the letters Vilma stole. You didn't really welcome love. Don't deny it! It is not enough to love somebody, you must love courageously. You must love so that no thief or plan or law, whether that be the law of heaven or of the world, can come between. The problem was that we did not love each other courageously enough. And that is your fault, because a man's courage in love is ridiculous.

Love is of your making. It is the only respect in which you achieve greatness. That is where, somehow, you fell short, and as you failed so did everything else, everything that might have been, all that was obligation, mission, the meaning of life. It is not true that men can be held responsible for this or that love. Go on, love heroically. But you committed the worst sin a woman can commit, you took offense, you ran away. Do you believe me yet?"

"What does all this add up to?" I asked. "What does it matter whether I believe or confess or resign myself?" My voice sounded so odd I might have overheard it in another room.

"That is why I have come," he said, more quietly now because the room had darkened and we instinctively dropped our voices as if everything—all the objects in the room, all we had to say—was fading with the light. "I wanted you to know," he went on, "that people can't end anything by simply wanting it to end, one can't abandon something before it has run its course. It is impossible!" he declared, and gave a satisfied laugh. I was half expecting him to rub his hands together like a card player who has, to his greatest astonishment, discovered that he has won a round he firmly expected to lose. "You are part of me, even now, when time and distance have annihilated all we once had together . . . Do you understand yet? You are responsible for everything that has happened in my life, just as I—in my fashion, in a man's fashion—am responsible for you, for your life. There was bound to come a day when you would know that. You must come away with me, with us. We'll take Nunu too. Listen, Esther, just this once you have to believe me. What possible advantage would I have in telling you anything but the truth, the last mortal truth? . . . Time burns away everything, everything that is false in us. What remains is the truth. And what remains is that you are a part of me even though you ran away, even though I was what I was and am. Yes, I too believe that people don't change. You are a part of me even though you know I have not changed, that I am the same as I was, as dangerous and unreliable. You cannot deny it. Raise your head, look into my eyes . . . Why won't you raise your head? Wait, I'll turn on the light . . . You still have no electricity? . . . Look, it is completely dark now."

He went over to the window, looked out, then closed it. But he did not light the table lamp. Instead he spoke to me in the darkness.

"Why won't you look at me?" he asked.

And when I did not answer, he went on in the murk, his voice farther away now.

"If you really are so absolutely convinced, why won't

you look at me? I have no kind of power over you. I have no rights. And yet there is nothing you can do against me. You can accuse me of anything you like, but you must know that you are the only person in the world before whom I am innocent. And there came a day, and it was I who returned. Do you still believe in words like 'pride'? Between people who are bound to each other by fate there is no pride. You will come with us. We will arrange everything. What will happen? We will live. Maybe life still has something in store for us. We will live quietly. The world has forgotten all about me. You will live there with me, with us. There's no other way," he said aloud, exasperated, as though he had finally understood and grasped something, something so simple, so blindingly obvious, that he resented arguing about it. "There's nothing else I want from you except that just this once, for the last time in your life, you should obey the law that is the meaning and the content of your life."

I could hardly see in the dark by now.

"Do you understand?" he asked, his voice quiet, coming at me from a long distance. It was as if he were talking to me out of the past.

"Yes," I said involuntarily, almost in a trance.

That was the moment the curious numbness started, the kind sleepwalkers must feel when setting out on their dangerous course; I understood everything that was happening around me, I was fully aware of what I was doing and saying, I saw people clearly, as well as those parts of their souls that manner and custom tend to draw a veil over, but knew at the same time that whatever I was doing so sensibly and so firm of purpose was to some degree unconscious, that it was partly a dream. I was calm, almost good-humored. I felt light, without a care. There was indeed something I understood that moment in Lajos's words, something stronger, more rational, more compelling than anything else, something over and above his charge against me. Naturally, I did not believe a word he said, but my skepticism amused me. While Lajos was speaking I understood something, the simple, assuring truth of which I could not have articulated in words. He was lying again, of course . . . I didn't quite know in what way or in what respect, but he was lying. Maybe it wasn't even his words or feelings that had lied, it might have been just his very being, the fact that he, Lajos, could not do anything else, not before and not now. Suddenly I was aware of myself laughing; I had burst into laughter, not a mocking laughter but a sincere, good-humored laughter. Lajos did not understand why I was laughing.

"Why are you laughing?" he asked suspiciously.

"It's nothing," I said. "Do please carry on."

"Do you agree?"

"Yes," I said. "To what? No, of course I agree," I quickly added.

"Good," he said. "In that case . . . Now look, Esther, you mustn't believe that anyone is against you or wishes you harm. We have to arrange our affairs as simply and as honorably as we can. You are coming with me. Nunu too . . . maybe not straightaway . . . a little later. Éva gets married. We have to redeem her," he said more quietly, as though we were plotting. "And me too . . . You can't understand it all yet . . . But do you trust me?" he asked uncertainly, his voice quiet.

"Carry on," I answered, just as quietly, joining the air of conspiracy. "Of course I trust you."

"That's most important," he muttered with satisfaction. "Don't think," he added more loudly, "that I will betray your trust. I don't want you to make a decision right away. There are just the two of us here. I'll go and call Endre. He is a family friend, a notary, with an official role. You should sign it in his presence," he declared with a large gesture.

"Sign what?" I asked him in the same conspiratorial tone, like someone who has agreed and volunteered for a task and is merely inquiring after details.

"This piece of paper," he said. "This contract that authorizes us to arrange everything and to have you come and live with us."

"With you?" I asked.

"With us," he said uncomfortably. "With us . . . Near us."

"Wait a minute," I said. "Before you call Endre . . . before I sign . . . Just clear up one matter for me. You want me to leave everything and go with you. I understand that much. But what happens after that? Where, near you, will I be living?"

"What we were thinking," he said slowly, turning the matter over in his mind as if it were perfectly normal, "was that it would be somewhere near us. Our apartment, unfortunately, is not suitable . . . But there is a home there where lonely ladies of a certain standing . . . It's quite close. And we could see each other often," he added generously, as if to encourage me.

"A sort of workhouse, I imagine?" I asked, perfectly calm.

"A workhouse?" he replied, wounded. "What an idea! A home, I said, with ladies of good upbringing. People like you and Nunu."

"Like me and Nunu," I said.

He waited a while longer. Then he went over to the table, found a match, and lit the table lamp with clumsy, unpracticed movements.

"Think it over," he said. "Think, Esther. I'll send Endre in. Think hard. And read the contract before signing it. Read it very carefully."

He produced a sheet of paper folded into four from his pocket and placed it modestly on the table. He looked me over one more time with a friendly encouraging smile, gave a little bow, and, sprightly as a young man, turned and left the room.

19

By the time Endre entered a few minutes later I had signed the contract that empowered Lajos to sell the house and garden. It was a proper contract, full of the proper terms, the text entirely composed of professional-sounding phrases, exactly like wills and marriages. Lajos had titled it "A two-party contract." I was one of the parties, Lajos the other, who in return for the rights to the estate comprising both house and garden contracted himself to look after Nunu and me. The details of the "looking after" were not indicated.

"Lajos has told me everything," said Endre once we had sat down, face-to-face, at the round table. "It is my duty to warn you, Esther, that Lajos is a scoundrel."

"Yes," I said.

"It is my duty to warn you that the terms and intentions of the contract he has sprung on you are dangerous and would be so even if Lajos followed those terms to the letter. You two, dear Esther, thanks to Nunu and the garden, have enjoyed a modest but stable existence here, and Lajos's plans sound, to a stranger's ear at least, a little sentimental . . . But I have no faith in Lajos's sentiments. I have known him, and known him well, for twenty-five years. Lajos is the sort of man, the sort of character, who does not change."

"No," I said. "He himself says he does not change."

"He says it too?" asked Endre. He took off his glasses and looked at me with his myopic eyes, blinking rapidly and clearly confused. "It doesn't matter what he says. He was sincere just now? Deeply sincere? It means nothing. I have had many sincere meetings with Lajos. Twenty years ago, if you recollect, Esther . . . for twenty years I have kept this quiet. But now is the time to tell you—twenty years ago when old Gábor, your father, dear Esther . . . forgive me, he was a good friend, a really close friend . . . in other words, twenty years ago when your father died and it fell to me, as his friend and the local notary, to conduct the bitter task of sorting out your estate, it turned out that Lajos had faked certain bills in the old man's name. Did you know about this?"

"Vaguely," I said. "There was some talk. But nothing was proved."

"But the point is that it could have been proved," he said and wiped his glasses. I had never seen him so confused. "There was documentary evidence to prove that Lajos had faked the bills. If we hadn't looked to it properly this house and this garden would not have remained yours, dear Esther. Now I can tell you. It was no easy matter . . . Enough to say I endured a 'sincere' interview with Lajos. I remember it very clearly, since it wasn't the kind of scene one is ever likely to forget. I repeat: Lajos is a scoundrel. I was the only one among you who did not fall under his spell. He knows that, he knows it very well . . . He is afraid of me. Now, when he breaks in on you and, to all intents and purposes, seems determined to rob you of everything that remains, to rob this modest little island with its crew of shipwrecked castaways of their peace and tranquility, it is my duty to warn you that that is the case. It is true that Lajos works more carefully now. He does not use bills. He seems to have been cornered somehow and can think of no other way of getting out but to come here to say good-bye and rob you of everything you have left . . . If you do sign over the house and garden to him there will be nothing I can officially do for you. Nobody can anyway. I alone could . . . that is, if you wanted me to."

"What can you do, Endre?" I asked, astonished.

He bent his head and gazed at his clumsy button-up shoes.

"Well, I . . ." he began, clearly embarrassed and reluctant. "You must know that at that time I was foolish and saved Lajos. I saved him from prison. How? It doesn't matter anymore. The bills had to be paid so you could remain in the house . . . It wasn't Lajos I wanted to save. Suffice to say the bills were paid. And you stayed here in peace without having to worry. I let Lajos run free. But the bills, all the evidence of the crime, I put away and kept. As far as the law is concerned the evidence is no longer valid. But Lajos knows that though he has escaped the clutches of the law he is still in my power. I beg you, dear Esther," he said almost ceremonially, and stood up, "empower me to talk to Lajos, to give him back this . . . this sheet of paper . . . and to send his people on their way. They would go if I insisted. Believe me," he said with satisfaction.

"I believe you," I said.

"In that case . . ." he said decisively and made to move.

"I believe you," I said quickly, with a catch in my throat. I knew that this was beyond Endre's understanding, that he could never resign himself to it, never really grasp it. "And I am most grateful . . . It is only now that I understand, and I am in no position to thank you. But that means that everything, everything that remained after Father's death, is ours thanks to you, dear Endre? If not for you, twenty years ago . . . then there would be no house, no garden, nothing. And everything would have been different, including my life . . . I would have had to live elsewhere, in some unknown place . . . Is that so?"

"Not entirely," he said, embarrassed. "It was not just me alone . . . Perhaps I can really tell you now. Tibor forbade me mentioning it before. He helped too. As an old friend of Gábor's he was only too happy and keen to help. We were all part of this . . ." he said, clearly in agonies, very quietly, his face red.

"Oh, Tibor," I said, and gave a nervous laugh. "So that's how it is. One lives in ignorance, not knowing that something bad, nor that something very good, has happened to one. It is impossible to render proper thanks for this. But it is even more difficult . . ."

"To send Lajos away?" he asked, looking serious.

"To send Lajos away," I mechanically repeated. "Yes, it will be very difficult now. He, of course, will leave immediately with his children and those strangers. They will soon set off, since they want to leave while it's light. Lajos will go. But the house and the garden . . . well, yes, I have given it all to him. I have signed this piece of paper . . . and I ask you, Endre, to talk to him and persuade him to look after Nunu. That is the one thing he must promise to do. You are right, of course, his promise is not worth anything, so this must be arranged in a proper legal manner, through some official contract, but a contract that will hold . . . He must reserve a proportion of the sale price for Nunu. She will not need very much now, poor thing. Can that be done?"

"Yes," he said. "We can do all that. But what about you, Esther? What will become of you?"

"Indeed. What will become of me? That's the whole point," I said. "Lajos suggested that I should leave this house and live somewhere near him . . . Not precisely with him . . . He did not go into detail about this. But that's not the important thing," I quickly said, seeing Endre frowning and raising his hand as if to interrupt me. "I want to explain this to you, Endre, to you and to Tibor, and to Laci as well, to all of you who have been so kind to us . . . I don't need to explain to Nunu, she understands . . . she is perhaps the only one who does in the end understand how everything must be done today precisely as it was twenty years ago. I think she might understand. I think only a woman could really understand this, the kind of woman who is no longer young and no longer expects anything from life . . . A woman like Nunu. A woman like me."

"I don't understand," he grumbled.

"I don't want you to understand," I said, and would have liked to hold his hand or touch his old gray-bearded face, that sad, wise, male face, a man's face, with my fingertips. I wanted to touch a man who had never pressed himself on me but whom I had to thank for twenty years of decent, honorable, humane life.

"You are a man, Endre, a splendid, true man, and are therefore obliged always to think rationally, the way the law or custom or reason wisely dictate. But we, we women, cannot be wise and rational in the same way . . . I understand now that that is not our affair. If I had been truly wise and honest twenty years ago I would have eloped from here with Lajos, my sister's fiancé, Lajos the swindler, the notorious liar, that piece of human garbage, as Nunu would put it since she likes to express herself forcefully. That is what I should have done had I been brave and wise and honest twenty years back . . . What would my fate have been? I don't know. I doubt it would have been particularly pleasant or cheerful. But at least I would have obeyed a law and fulfilled an obligation that is stronger than the laws of reason and the world generally . . . Do you understand now? Because I have come to understand . . . I have understood it to the point that I am giving Lajos and Éva the house because it is what I owe them . . . And then . . . what will be will be."

"You are going to leave?" he quietly asked.

"I don't know," I said, suddenly exhausted. "I haven't worked out what should happen to me yet. In any case I ask you to give Lajos this piece of paper—yes, I have signed it—and I want you, Endre, to add a tough and binding codicil to ensure that the pitiful amount remaining to Nunu should not fall into Lajos's hands. Do you promise?"

He made no answer to my question. He picked up the contract between two fingers, as if it were a dirty, suspicious object.

"Yes, all right," he sighed. "Of course, I knew nothing of this."

I caught his hand but immediately let it go.

"Forgive me," I said, "but no one in twenty years has asked me about it. Not you, not Tibor . . . Maybe I myself was less certain, Endre, was less so bitterly certain that Lajos was right in saying that there is a kind of invisible order in life and that what one has begun one has also to end . . . As and when . . . Well, now that's done with," I said, and stood up.

"Yes," he said, the sheet in his hand, his head bowed. "It is probably superfluous to say it, but should you regret this . . . either now or in the future . . . we are always here, Tibor and I."

"It is indeed superfluous," I said, and tried to smile.

20

*A*bout midnight I heard Nunu's footsteps; she climbed slowly up the creaking, rotted wooden stairs, pausing on every third step to cough. She stopped on the threshold of my room just as she had last night, the flickering candle in her hand, wearing her day clothes, the solitary black ceremonial dress she had not yet had time to take off.

"You're not asleep," she said, and sat down beside me on the bed, placing what remained of the candle on the bedside table.

"You know they have even taken the jam?"

"No," I said. I sat up in the bed and started laughing.

"Not everything, just the peach," she said in a matter-of-fact way. "All twenty jars. Éva asked for them. They took the flowers, too, the remaining dahlias in the garden. It doesn't matter. They would have faded by next week anyway."

"Who took the flowers?" I asked.

"The woman."

She coughed, folded her arms, and sat up straight, as calm and self-contained as ever in life, whatever the situation. I took her bony hand that was neither warm nor cold.

"Let them take what they want, Nunu," I said.

"Of course," she agreed. "Let them take it, my girl. If there's no alternative."

"I couldn't go down to supper," I said, and squeezed her hand for support. "Don't be cross. Were they not surprised?"

"No, they were simply quiet. I don't think they were surprised."

We both looked at the unsteady candle flame. I felt cold.

"Nunu, darling," I asked her. "Please close the shutters. And there, on the sideboard, you'll find three letters. Would you bring them over, my dear?"

She moved slowly through the room, her shadow enormous on the wall. She closed the windows and brought over the letters, then she tucked me up and sat back down beside me, her arms folded, a touch ceremonially in her ceremonial dress, as if appearing at some peculiar, grotesque occasion, an occasion unlike others, one that was neither wedding nor funeral. She sat and listened.

"Do you understand, Nunu?" I asked her.

"Yes, my girl, I understand. I understand," she said, and put her arms around me.

So we sat and waited for the candle to burn down or for the wind to abate, the wind that had been moaning around the house ever since midnight, tearing at the muddy boughs of the trees, waiting perhaps for morning. I myself didn't know what we were waiting for. I shivered.

"You are tired," she said, and covered me up.

"Yes," I said. "I am very tired. It was all too much, you know. I'd like to sleep, Nunu dear. Would you be so kind as to read me those three letters?"

She reached into her apron pocket, searched for her wire-framed spectacles, and carefully studied the letters.

"Lajos wrote them," she said.

"You recognize his writing?"

"Yes. Have you only just received them?"

"Just now."

"When did he write them?"

"Twenty years ago."

"Is it the fault of the mail that they have just been delivered? . . ." she asked, partly curious, partly jealous.

"No, not the mail," I smiled.

"Whose fault was it?"

"Vilma's."

"She stole them? . . ."

"She stole them."

"I see," she said, and sighed. "I hope she rests in peace. I never did like her."

She adjusted the glasses on her nose, leaned to the flame, and began to read one of the letters as if she were back at school, quietly, in a singsong voice.

" 'My one and only darling,' " she read, " 'life is playing extraordinary tricks on us. I have no other hope but that I should have found you forever . . .' "

She stopped reading, pushed the glasses up to her forehead, and turned to me with shining eyes, moved and enchanted.

"He certainly could write a wonderful letter!"

"Yes," I agreed. "Read on. He was a brilliant letter writer."

But the wind, the end-of-September wind that had until then been snapping at the walls of the house, suddenly tore open the window, billowed through the curtains, and, as if it were bringing news, touched and shifted everything in the room. Then it blew out the candle flame. I still remember that. And remember also, though only vaguely, that at some stage Nunu closed the window, and I fell asleep.